CLOUDS OF FIRE

A NOVEL BY
LU JONES WAITE

based on the screenplay by
Alan Foote and Craig Holyoak

Randall Publishers

International Standard Book No. 0-934126-20-8

First Printing March 1981.

Randall Publishers
93 South Mountainway Drive
Orem, Utah 84057

Printed in the United States of America
Publishers Press
Salt Lake City, Utah

Dedicated to the memory of those downwind people who have suffered.

Appreciation is extended to Kirk Tanner for editorial and conceptual assistance.

CONTENTS

PREFACE

Downwind is about a time in America when concerns for America seemed more important than concerns for some of her people. It is a fictional story based on actual events that occurred in the Southwest United States during the 1950's and 1960's. During those years, the United States, under the direction of the Atomic Energy Commission (A.E.C.), conducted approximately 84 atmospheric nuclear tests in the Nevada test site, just eighty miles north of Las Vegas and 140 miles southwest of St. George, Utah.

The A.E.C. claimed at the time, and still asserts, that it did everything possible to insure the safety of not only the test site employees but of the citizens in surrounding towns and cities during the tests. They also assured the public that what they knew about nuclear fallout indicated there was no cause to believe there was danger to anyone from nuclear effects. There is, however, reason to doubt the validity of both claims made at the time by the A.E.C. Tests, for example, were not conducted when the prevailing winds would carry the fallout in the direction of Las Vegas or Los Angeles. The devices were exploded instead when the winds carried the radiation in the direction of Arizona and Southern Utah. The people in those areas were then advised simply to stay indoors for one hour.

Scientists once employed by the A.E.C. now say that the government agency knew a great deal more about fallout than they claimed. Evidence obtained from the war and animal tests showed the A.E.C. more about the hazards of nuclear contamination than they admit knowing in the 1950's.

It appears that citizens of the United States were innocent participants in a program to improve America's atomic capacities and have been repaid with abnormally high rates of bone cancer, leukemia, and thyroid cancer that are taking their toll. *Downwind* portrays some of the concerns and suffering of these victims who can explain their dilemma only in terms of nuclear contamination.

Although it is the people of Southwestern United States that have born the weight of what some see as government indifference and others as miscalculation, *Downwind* is a story of national and world-wide appeal. This issue has received national attention when a United States Senate committee, headed by Senator Edward Kennedy, heard testimony from witnesses claiming government cover-up and neglect. A Utah congressman has since introduced legislation for compensation by the federal government for victims of nuclear testing.

There are 965 claims now pending in federal court by victims and survivors from the fallout regions seeking damages in excess of two billion dollars.

CHAPTER 1

Sarah Collins had always pampered her family. As she walked back to the house, arm in arm with her husband Jedediah, the bubbling life within her couldn't be contained. Stopping quickly, she brought him about and faced him. Wrapping her arms about her husband, her merry, velvety eyes snapped. "Jed, have I told you today that I love you?"

"Just never quit, woman. It's your loving faith that makes the sun shine for me. Remember it's an old man you're loving." Jed loved taunting her and placing his usual peck on her brow. He smiled.

"Old? Shame on you, Jedediah Collins; fifty-two years is just starting to really live! Your father was past ninety-eight when he died, your mother eighty-six; oh, darling, let's still have years and years together, please!" She hugged him hard, and taking him by the hand, walked along at his side.

As they neared the house, it seemed as if two roaring cyclones whirled from it and were heading straight for them.

"We've set the table as you asked, Mom, and we're hungry," blurted young Jenny while clinging breathlessly to her father. Jeremy, the other half of the cyclone, skillfully nudged in between his parents.

"Daddy, we're going to Aunt Pal's tonight, aren't we? I want to hear the music again!" Jenny's face gleamed hopefully. "It's our turn to have the Granny Band here next, isn't it? Aunt Pal plays the guitar and sings, doesn't she? They're all old, aren't they?" The perplexity upon her small face and all her questions made them laugh.

"Honey," Sarah smiled, "grannies are supposed to be old; they have grandchildren you know."

"But they make beautiful sounds!" Jenny swished away from her father, waving her arms and twisting her young body. "It makes people dance, like this." The child's sweet movements made the couple smile.

"Yes, we'll drive into St. George tonight, and I love the music just as much as you do, Jenny," Jed replied as he saw the delight in his daughter's smile.

"Are you and Mama going to dance the quadrille?" Jeremy ventured in a solemn voice. "Mama, are you going to wear your pretty whirly dress?"

"Sure she is!" Jenny interjected. "Papa will wear the shirt Mama made him, too. They go together, don't they, Mama?"

"Yes, love, they go together. And about dancing, if your father isn't too tired."

"Tired? What's that, woman? Just start up the Granny Band, and I'm ready to swing my partner and do-si-do." Jed's antics as he swung his wife made the twins laugh.

That night on the drive to Aunt Pal's the darkness of the still desert night fell smoothly, and the smiling face of the man in the moon reflected down its subtle radiance.

The moon-lit vermillion hills of Utah looked shaggy, with spook caves, witches, and goblins to young Jenny. To Jeremy's straining eyes, the moon revealed only glimpses of horses,

2

bandits, and Indians. But to the mother, as they drove down the road, the night touched her world. The enchanting red hills evoked memories in her, long since dormant. She remembered the walks taken at night, back in the yesteryears, the cooling breeze that had made her lover's hand clasp warm, the whispering slow motion of a small town going to sleep, the dearness of Jed the night they had stood at the very top of the red hill, letting their eyes linger upon the magic of the lighted town below. The moon that night, Sarah remembered, was just as it was tonight, a splendid thing of glory. How utterly magical she had felt then when his voice, so dear, so full of love, had asked her to marry him.

The black hills and grudging land, too, held cherished memories for her. It had been a barren waste before the pioneers had come in the 1850's, and though a river had to be outsmarted with canals built for irrigation and suitable crops found for the bedouin climate and the parched, brackish soil, it was still her land; the land of four generations inbedded in her blood. The same feelings were even more so with Jed, for his thoughts were those of the tiller of the soil.

Sarah stole her husband's hand and with it caressed her cheek. Her silent love oozed out and up into the very depths of Jedediah's soul. His hand jerked, then drew her to him.

"Woman, do you want to wreck this car?" he chided.

"Jed Collins, all I want is to be near you." Her smile was gentle. "It's such a beautiful night!"

"Yes. We've been down this trail before, Sarah." He relaxed and let go part of the tension he refused to accept.

"I know, my love, I was just reminiscing." Suddenly her voice was electrified. "Jedediah, do you know it was on this date a little over thirty years ago in 1926 that you finally broke down

3

and asked me to marry you?"

"Woman, woman, how you frightened me." His voice was jocular. "I didn't want to be turned down, and your parents, bless their hearts, were so correct in all things. I was sure they wouldn't take me into their family."

"How self-righteous you thought we were," laughed Sarah.

As Jed and Sarah parked the car and joined the crowd on the large back lawn of Sarah's Aunt Pal, their faces beamed; friends from forty to fifty miles away and even more greeted them.

"Just can't beat your Granny Band. They make all bones jingle. Especially old bones, eh, Jed?" Chuck Haynes extended a familiar rough hand.

"That's right, Chuck. And what would we do without our square dancing?" Jed came back at him.

"It's a corker the way these old timers can ring music out of the pitchfork I use in my hay field," Chuck said, grinning widely. "And here comes your aunt with the washboard and the saw! How they make them talk I'll never know!" A twinkle danced in Chuck's eyes.

"It runs hot in the blood of my wife's family. It's their daily diet." Jed's chest expanded.

"They say your young daughter is a wonder at the piano," Chuck mused.

"She's beyond my comprehension, but Sarah understands her. They understand each other, and I suppose that's the secret," Jed smiled.

"Doesn't surprise me how come we have to fight to get a seat here or wherever these oldies play. We live from month to month just to come," Chuck's voice was gleeful. "Here we come seventy-five miles just for upliftings that carry us along for a month, just to come again; others have come from forty to fifty miles."

"Yes, and did you know the Granny Band is going to Salt Lake City to play?" Jed's eyes sought his wife's whereabouts. "You know, Chuck, it's always been this way with us around here. Simple people just wanting a little security, giving what we have for peace and happiness.

"Well, here they go Collins; get your partner. Let's swing um high — yip-e-ye and a do-si-do." Chuck Haynes' voice filled the air, and his antics, as his arms went up and as he two-stepped away from Jed, brought a roar from the crowd. He always brought happiness with him.

The dancers formed four circles with four in each. And at the first strum on the electric guitar, each Granny member made ready to go.

For four hours the quadrilles, schottische, polkas, and other old time dances made the night air in St. George ring.

A long standing custom, each to bring a favorite dish, or pot luck as it was called, made the night more enjoyable, with no heavy burden put upon anyone. And it was open-house to those who wished to stay overnight. This night the Haynes' were to be tucked away in the hospitality of Jedediah and Sarah Collins' home, and life would be made richer for both.

As goodnights were being said, Rod Meyer came toward them, limping and laughing.

"Funny thing what this Granny Band does to me. The minute the band strikes up my crutches go into a corner. I don't even think of them again until I'm ready to leave."

Jed and Chuck laughed with him. Then Chuck grinned jauntily and pointed toward the punch bowl. "He isn't the only old man who forgets his crutches and his aches. Look at Bert

Watson and Chester Boles there. Aren't they both in their eighties?"

"Yes, one is eighty-six, the other eighty-three. I believe Rod is eighty-five." Jed always prided himself on his memory.

"Anyone get the ten o'clock news?" a loud voice asked. "Stay in-doors tomorrow, the wind is blowing our way; no danger, but. . . ," the voice lowered to a strident pitch. "It's blowing away from Los Angeles and Vegas, but St. George, Enterprise, New Castle, and other small towns must take what comes."

Job Stringer's voice boomed, "Keep the kids in when the cloud comes; at daybreak the shot goes off. And by the way, folks, how can we bring our cows into the house? We *do* drink the milk and eat the meat."

Jed Collins recoiled, his fists clenched. Job Stringer, or any other man, didn't have the right to put a death knell to such a beautiful evening. He moved away, his eyes dulled a little, and his shoulders drooped. He sensed the growing tension among the people and wasn't himself easy in his own thoughts anymore, for untold things were happening, and the thunder of dissension had started to roll.

Jed gathered his family and friends close, wanting to preserve some of the happiness of the night.

Driving home started out in silence, but Sarah's bubbling nature couldn't be repressed.

"Tonight was too much for you, Jed! Next time we won't dance so much."

"Woman," Jed's eyes were grave as he looked at her moonbeamed face, "I think your perceptive eye could calculate a wrong number once in a while. I love to swing you high."

"I know, and I love you to sweep me off my feet," her eyes glowed. "But, dear, I love you far above dancing or worldly goods — you come first, you know." She snuggled close to him. "It's such a beautiful night."

Jed loved her closeness and treasured the years he had her love. Staring into the night, he thanked the powers that were for his children — even the son who had expelled himself from the good earth he loved so dearly, to take up another life, foreign to him, but exciting and alluring to his son. An unconscious sigh quivered his body, and instantly the woman beside him whispered.

"Jedediah, dear, we both love him, and he *is* a good son."

"Sarah, I pity the person who tries to deceive you. Yes, it was Brady I was thinking about."

"I know, dear, and even though we gave birth to him, we couldn't mold his heart — to have controlled him by force would have killed him and us." Sarah laid a handful of tenderness on his arm. "We have each other and the twins." She turned to look at the two sleeping mounds on the back seat. "Jed, we both can see the yearnings of the soil starting to seep into Jeremy's young bones, and his love for the animals grows every day. You truly have a farmer in a son, Jed. It will all work out. We must have faith in what's happening around us."

"Then Job's remarks did upset you, Sarah?" he spoke low.

"Yes," she confessed. "I, too, have my feelings, dear, and I'll keep a better watch on those I love."

"Woman," he drew her close. "I do love you."

CHAPTER 2

Southern Utah mornings are beautiful as only crisp desert mornings can be. The occasional bark of the coyote, the whisper of a gentle wind, the sleeping desert heat put to rest only to be awakened when the sun's rays emerge, making the desert yield up the ghosts of cities, mountains, lakes. All work in unison to create a vision of stark beauty.

But this morning, as a plane took to the sky its occupants, Captain Jerry Wilson and Captain Jim Baker beheld a different sight. A particular area was now completely devastated of its beauty from the heat and deadly gamma ray radiation of many atom bomb tests which had obliterated all life within a fifty mile radius.

"Nothing like a desert sunrise. Just look to the east, pal. No doubt where the east is either." The pilot's voice was full of awe. "Look way over towards Mount Charleston. The lush green is quite a contrast. Vegas, too, is lit up like day. Too bad this little sleeping town below us won't be here tomorrow."

"Yah, this mission isn't to my liking," Jim, the co-pilot, answered with reservation.

"I wouldn't want to be in its path. Can't tell me that cloud loses its potency as long as it drifts in the sky," remarked the pilot. "Just look at that sky! I'd say it's an atom bomb itself."

"I'd say so, and Jerry, this atom stuff we're fooling with, it scares me."

"Yah, I agree with you." Captain Wilson paused, looking out the cockpit windows. "Look at those colors! There's the Pahranagat Range of mountains and the old Sheep Mountain, too — the kiss of life they're getting this morning won't be forgotten for awhile."

"You and your old paint brush — all you can see is colors, colors, colors!" the co-pilot jested.

"Well, isn't it so? Just look below you now. . . ," the pilot's voice was excited. "See the colors, and even the ground looks different where the bomb hasn't been dropped."

"Yah, you're right. Jerry, how long is this valley that the test site surrounds anyway?" His companion was serious.

"Uh, I dunno. It's one hundred and fifty miles from Tonopah to Mercury, and that's only one small side. Frenchman Flat, where the bomb drops today, is just a dot on the map in comparison to the whole area." There was a pause. "Look below. See the control point? You can recognize it by the airstrip and helicopter pad. Look! There's the trailer complex and the fuel storage tanks."

"Sure can, and it's quite a place, isn't it?" Jim looked below.

"Alpha 7, come in — do you read me?" The voice came clear to the pilot.

"Mother, this is Alpha 7. Read you loud and clear," the pilot answered. "We have a go on this end. T minus 10 minutes and go for final countdown. Mark — now."

Below, at Command Point, General George Freeman, along with high ranking army personnel, technicians, scientists, and reporters watched the large bomber overhead.

"Mother, this is Alpha 7. We are nearing point of no return. Do you read me?" Captain Wilson waited for reply and checked all points essential to their mission.

"Quite a town below and to think we have to catch them unaware." The pilot pointed below. "Huh, got a live presence there. See that coyote?"

"Where? Oh, I see it. He's never gonna know what hit him," the co-pilot laughed. "Light enough now to see the town pretty good. Even the service station and cars."

"Mother, this is Alpha 7. Repeat — We are nearing point of no return. Do you read me?" Captain Wilson rechecked to confirm all instructions.

"Alpha 7, this is Mother. We have you two minutes, repeat, two minutes from ground zero. . . ."

The pilot eased the bomber to the correct altitude. "Mother, this is Alpha 7. We have ground zero in T minus thirty seconds." The pilot instructed the co-pilot, "Make all points ready to go."

"Mother, fifteen seconds to ground zero. We are T minus 10, 9, 8, 7, 6. . . ."

Below the coyote turned, hesitated, then moved on down the street.

"— 5, 4, 3, 2, 1 — The bomb's away!" Then the connections were cut off.

The bomber shot out and up, but the coyote and the sleepy townspeople were unprepared for the approaching doom. Again the coyote stood motionless as a porch swing squeaked in the breeze, and the curtains at a kitchen window billowed slightly out.

As if by magic, the calm of the desert suddenly exploded!

There was a burning, rocking inferno below, its horrendous results spreading rapidly.

The coyote was flung across the street, as uncontrollable as a piece of paper in a tornado. The explosive burst caused a white heat that consumed everything in its path. Houses fell apart and burst into flames. The earth rocked and waved like a turbulent sea. The sleeping occupants of one house were dashed violently across the room as furniture and all things flew in the same direction. In the children's rooms the bunk beds split apart, and the children were thrown across the room, their bodies twisted and bent grotesquely. In the nursery the wall crashed inward onto the crib as the brick, crib, and baby flew across the room and through an adjacent wall.

Outside, two men at a gas station seemed transfixed, and a telephone pole, as moveable as a match stick, came hurling at them. Both were blown away together. The wind roared, the noise crescendoed into a savage vengeance, tossing cars and every conceivable thing as if they were mere toys.

The destruction was tremendous and kept spreading rapidly. The buildings on the outskirts of the town were almost obscured by dust and debris from shattered houses.

A heavy cloud hovered over the town, its orange-purplish-red color expanding above the searing inferno below. The cloud rose and mushroomed out, and the wind current started to move it in a northeasterly direction.

At the same time, Control Point excitement mounted. As the bomb exploded, the men at the control panels watched intently as the information was measured and recorded. General George Freeman, his staff, and state officials were there to witness the actual explosion and were well pleased at the results achieved. Especially pleased was the ever-smiling General

Freeman himself. His stocky, five-eleven stance and two hundred and twenty pound frame seemed taller at that moment. His face, made ruddy by the heat, and his mouth, pulled straight yet betraying signs of weakness, simpered and smirked with self-importance. It was the eyes though, almost colorless in their blue-white steeliness, that spoke most eloquently of his arrogance. His superficial charm had wooed and won the most beautiful of women and had turned the heads of states and kingdoms. Now he was out to captivate and lull the unsuspecting, ignorant populace of this sparsely inhabited area into believing that the fallout from the atomic blasts was not harmful. His ego was mountainous, and the magnitism of his personality made him almost irresistible. His almost white hair, touched by a burnish red tint, climaxed his carefully contrived appearance.

Rubbing his hands in a gloating way, his voice, smooth as honey, brought approval from the members of the group. That is, all but one, Dr. Charity Fuller.

"Ah, such overwhelming success — such superb timing!" the general exclaimed.

"Yes, the wind is at its best, General Freeman. Away from Las Vegas and California, but what about the smaller towns in its path?" Dr. Fuller cut the general short.

"Of no consequence, my dear Charity. As I've said before, it is of no consequence," his voice humored her. "By the time the cloud drifts that far there are no worries."

"It's Dr. Fuller to you, General Freeman. There's no need to play cat-and-mouse with me either." Dr. Fuller drew herself up to full height. Her five-foot ten-inch body was superbly chisled, curved, and contoured to bewitch the male eye. Though the woman was clothed in a researcher's gown, the effect was still there. Her dark red hair coiled in thick, luxuriant braids, wound twice about a shapely head, framed a face that showed character as well as beauty. Her dark eyes held a nebulous glint that kept everyone silently wondering what went on behind those mirrors of the soul.

From his first eye level look at the woman, General Freeman had in his conquering mind labeled her as his own. For Charity, however, the chemical reaction nauseated her completely. Yet her icy looks only served to spur the hunter to the chase. Freeman's conceit took on a facetious daring that came from having never been denied and so goaded him on.

"The day will come, Fuller. . . ," mused the general.

Charity Fuller stiffened, and her usually soft eyes froze. Suddenly changing her mind she walked away, her breath too precious to waste.

"Can't win 'em all, General," chided a voice from the group. A twitter went around the room.

"Perhaps. . . ." Freeman licked his lips. "Dr. Fuller is still under my command, and I crack the whip! There's time — plenty of time yet — and the pretty doctor stays."

CHAPTER 3

After the detonation, the Nevada desert had less activity than usual. Because another test shot had been released, the usual restrictions were enforced to keep men holed up for hours after each shot before entering their areas of work.

The desert looked normal, sunbleached, barren, and dry. But another death knell had been added to the already searing desert, one of man-made devastation.

The desert air had thickened for a time by a ferocious wind, blinding light, and a consuming heat. But now a semblance of calm pervaded the immediate compound as men at the test site in the Nevada desert, or as commonly called Nevada Proving Grounds, started to move about. With security outfits, white overalls, hoods, air masks, cameras, and flashlights they searched through the basements of the houses throughout the demolished town.

"Harold, hey Harold, you can't get away from us," quipped Dave Williams as he searched a basement. "You may be buried under all this rubble, but we'll find you yet."

"Maybe he flew the coop," grunted Ted Jones as he joined his companion. "The velocity of that little breeze from the blast could have torn him to shreds. Besides, the white hot heat burned things up pretty much."

"Nah," Williams grunted. "Harold wouldn't take unnecessary risks; he'd stay put."

"But, Dave, we've found the others — that is most — some in bits and pieces." Ted was anxious to be gone.

"Here's Harold! I told you we'd find him," Williams asserted.

Ted looked down upon an exposed arm, and together they dug out the person called Harold.

"Ted, go find the other crew members while I take a few pictures and make a few notes. Then we'll load 'um up and get out of here."

As Ted emerged into the open, he saw other crew members dressed as he was working among the debris. Close by a large, high-sided truck with severed arms and legs and with some partial and other complete corpses extending from it, stood waiting.

Before Ted could return, Dave appeared carrying Harold over his shoulder. As he approached the truck, Ted helped him lift the body into the truck.

"Did we get most of them?" Ted showed no emotion.

"Not as many as last time, but I've told the others to head back — too hot yet; we'll try again tomorrow." Dave got behind the wheel, and they moved out of the hot zone.

"Hey, we've lost a passenger. Harold wants to be unruly," Ted noticed.

Dave backed the truck up, and both got out and walked to the body. Picking it up, they coolly tossed it into the back with the others. Suddenly, for a split second, they both froze as the head fell off and rolled to the side of the road.

"Man, that threw me for a sec, Ted."

"That mannequin is a gory sight. Look at his face melted and scarred. He sure isn't the Harold of yesterday." Ted shivered slightly. "They're just bits and pieces mostly."

"Better mannequins than people." Dave seemed in deep thought and spoke mechanically.

"Yeah, and I wonder about the little towns and ranches close by. Some are not over fifty miles from here, other. . . ."

"We aren't being paid for thinking. Let's be on our way." Dave cut Ted off, but he couldn't stop his own thinking.

At a long table in the consultation room, men and women sat, expectancy written upon some faces, uncertainty on others; and on one, Dr. Charity Fuller, one of the head scientists at the atomic test site, apprehension.

As Mark Trevor, the main supervisor, began to speak, all eyes, except Charity's, were upon him.

"Ladies and gentlemen, it's with complete confidence, and. . . ." Trevor's eyes circled the room, his voice almost with self-importance, "I can say with great pleasure and the utter most confidence, all objectives were accomplished, and everything went as planned." A frown creased his brow as he looked at the side view of Dr. Fuller.

Charity Fuller was speculating upon the faces before her, trying to estimate the percentage of those who had reservations about what they were doing.

"Now," his voice boomed, and Fuller looked squarely at him, "we are waiting for some of the participants from the towns to be decontaminated. But while we wait, we have a film of the test, which I'm sure will thrill you since you are all part of the team that brought about its success. If you'll turn around. . . ."

Charity turned, scrutinizing the audience. Army brass, government agents, atomic personnel, advisors, researchers, scientists, men, and women — they were all there. Murmurs and excited comments were audible in praise of the complete demolition seen.

The reactions of her co-workers sickened Charity, and nausea tore through her inner self. It was too distressing for her; if only her voice could be heard, even by a few.

As the lights came on, Mark Trevor's voice was facetious. "If there are any questions. . . ."

"What happens to the radioactive fallout in that cloud we so successfully created?" Charity's voice was harsh and loud. She faced Trevor squarely.

A hushed silence filled the room.

"Dr. Fuller, I'm sure you know that the cloud is dispersed by the wind and that any waste material. . . ." Charity cut him short.

"And what happens to the people who live under that cloud?" Charity retorted. No one spoke for a time.

Finally, Trevor broke the silence. "And who would that be?" A cocky leer spread over his red face.

"Well, not your father and mother perhaps. But at least ten thousand unsuspecting, innocent people, and some not over sixty miles from here." Her voice held firm. "Southern Utah, some parts of Nevada, and Arizona reveal alarming high fallout levels. And yet some of us here are too careless in giving actual facts — or should I bluntly say some are trying to play God and let nothing but nothing, not even the sanctity of life, stand in the way of personal success. Don't deny it; I know. I see the reports."

"Dr. Fuller must be referring to St. George, which we alerted this morning." A suave voice cooled the room, and all eyes looked relieved as the cat-faced Freeman stood debonairly leaning in the doorway. "We've been over this before, Dr. Fuller." The General moved around the table and took a seat by the standing supervisor. "I really don't think we should waste time haggling over radiation levels in the cloud path when you know St. George is receiving no significant. . . ."

Just then Dave Williams burst into the room, cutting Freeman short.

"The decontamination is complete, sir, and the mannequins are here."

"Thank you, Williams. Bring them in, please; we are ready." A look of quiet relief covered Trevor's face as the remains of the mannequins were wheeled in. Harold's headless body came in last.

The occupants of the room wandered to the racks, and Trevor again began to speak. "The thing to notice first is the thermal effects on the different clothing types and color. . . ."

Charity Fuller sat listening to the presentation. She turned her head casually away and found Freeman staring at her, his eyes almost white in their steeled glare. A menacing glitter covered his face as his fixed, baby-faced smile ridiculed her.

Charity tried to choke back her anger, but the frustration she felt brought her to her feet, and the droning voice of the supervisor followed her down the hall.

"Notice the white clothing is least effected. . . ."

"Why, that low-down, no-good panther. I'd like to punch his smiling, rosy face to smithereens." Charity's hands were hard fists now, ready for combat. Trying to forget, throwing herself completely into her work, the anger subsided. As she made ready to leave for the night, a messenger came into her office grinning and raising his eyebrows.

"Dr. Fuller, General Freeman wants to see you in his office right away." Somewhat gauking, he surveyed her approvingly and added half kidding, "Some men have all the luck."

"Yes, well why don't you try your luck sometime, Cash. I wouldn't bet on the fair haired General." Her mischievous smile brought a whistle from Cash. "Thanks anyway, and I'm on my way."

Charity's step was much quieter now, and the messenger's teasing had broken the hardness of her face. She quietly opened Freeman's door and looked in.

"Yes, what is it, Fuller?" A coy smugness almost broke the steel in his eyes.

"*You* wanted to see *me*, sir," replied Charity, instantly raising her defenses.

"So I did. Yes, well, come in and shut the door." The General got to his feet, trying to stretch another inch, a false smile upon his countenance. "Do sit down," he cleared his throat while at the same time nervously chafing his hands.

"My dear Charity," he continued, "your concern for the farmers — the backwoodsmen shall we say — is quite commendable, in fact quite touching. It is a true reaction of a good woman."

"Come to the point, General. Let's not play games with each other. Your act gets you nowhere with me."

"All right, Fuller. As I've told you before, your meddling in my affairs has gone far enough. For the last time let me emphasize, *your fears* for the people in St. George or any town are unjustified. Your attitude is causing problems for me, and I want it stopped." Freeman stormed about the room, angered to white heat.

"As we are being honest, sir, let's face up to a few facts."

Charity jumped to her feet. "You know and I know that you are playing war games. But this time not with an enemy but with innocent people. The deadly results that you are keeping a tight lid on will cause innocent people for generations to die from the effects of the so called 'nothing to fear tests' you have so cleverly dismissed."

"Doctor Fuller, you are out of line. There never has been substantial evidence that people will die. . . ," Freeman never finished his sentence.

"And I say, Freeman, you're a liar!" She stood her ground.

"Well, my dear Charity," his cunning made her blaze, "you're getting a little hostile, aren't you?"

Charity faced the man down.

"Angry, yes, but lack of evidence? No! What about the reports of Doctors Finn, Wilcox, Mathews, and Sheldon? They show radiation levels in the clouds that blow over the unsuspecting people to be high. In fact, their reports state they don't even know just what a safe level is."

"My good woman, those reports were dismissed," Freeman leered defiantly.

"Dismissed!" Charity steamed. "Why? So you could continue the cash flow for these tests? So you could add another medal to your already speckled suit?" Charity thrust the newspaper she had in her hand at the General. "What about this? This paper runs a story and picture showing sheep bleeding at the nose. Farmers and sheepmen are losing sheep by the thousands. And you so innocently dismiss this by saying, 'It's purely coincidental.' Yet, General, the radiation level in the grass those sheep fed on was reported by *your people* to have been higher than at first calculated. In fact, the Atomic Energy Commission officials checked the dead animals with a geiger counter and pronounced them to be as hot as a two dollar pistol. And you, Freeman, stand there and *try* to tell me there is no danger!"

"Fuller, I'm warning you. . . ," his cool all but evaporated. "I'll have no more of this. You stick to your areas of concern, and we will get along fine. Step over your boundaries again and we may have some problems; do I make myself clear?"

"Why you. . . ." Charity straightened to full height. "Freeman, your rancid behavior makes you unbearable. Good night!" She left the dumbfounded general quickly.

CHAPTER 4

The day was rapidly fading into night as the black of the sky calmly blanketed a world going to sleep. The evening stars shined so bright and large it seemed as if they could be plucked from the sky.

This night the tang of new mown hay put an invigorating lift into the breathing of Sarah Collins, and her emotions fairly burst from excitement.

"Oh, Jed!" Sarah cried, embracing her husband. "I do love this time of the night! Just listen to the whispering of the trees on the breeze." Sarah playfully entwined her arms about his neck and raised her lips to be kissed. "Just listen to the gurgling of the water in the canal as it goes dancing over the rocks, bringing life to our land."

"Woman, you make it sound so easy. No toil, no struggle, no worry!" Looking into her upturned face, he studied it minutely. "Yes, we are lucky to have this land, ample water, and good climate. I, too, love its fertility and peacefulness. But above all I am blessed with you and the twins." Jed turned, looking into the fading west.

"Jedediah, there are three children." Sarah held her breath.

Then, with a slight rebuke in her voice, tried to reach her disgruntled husband. "It really isn't Brady, is it? These nuclear tests are bringing changes, aren't they?"

"So you say, woman. But Brady doesn't really care, and I'll not have you fretting about things you cannot help. We still have each other." He pulled her to him. "It's just that I'm getting old, I guess."

"Oh, not that again, too. You know it isn't age." She scrutinized his countenance. Noticeable changes of weariness and frustration were slowly etching away at the robust, apple-cheeked man she loved more than herself. To hide her tears, she looked faintly into the dimming night.

"Now, Sarah, don't carry on so." He turned her to him and wiped away a tear gently sliding down her cheek. "I'm not a dead man yet." He tried to joke, but the truth glared too openly. "Come, we must be going inside; the youngsters will be coming after us." Wrapping his arms around her shoulders, he guided her through the door.

"Please, will you go to Doctor Mac soon?" She trembled in his arms.

"If it pleases you, Sarah, but it will be useless."

"Mama, Mama," Jenny danced to her mother with eyes as big as plums. "We're to be kept in again tomorrow; it's another bomb! Do you think it will be pretty and come over St. George again?"

She hugged her child close. "I hope not, my darling, but come, it's time to be thinking about bed."

The night was restless for Sarah, and when the clock chimed four, she pulled herself out of bed, trying not to disturb her husband.

"Where are you going?" Jed's voice was rather hoarse.

"I — I couldn't sleep; it's about time for the bomb. I'd like to be up in case the children are aroused." Sarah held her fears in.

"You can't move mountains, Sarah; what is to come will come." Throwing off the covers, he went to her. "I couldn't sleep either. Just as well go milk the cows and get an early start on the hay." He forced a smile. "One good thing coming from these blasted tests — it's making early risers out of the slow farmers."

Too early for Sarah to start her work for the day, she followed her husband to the barn. It seemed but minutes later when the sky exploded, and the barn was bright as day.

"Jed, isn't there danger of the earth slipping in all this shaking? They say the Wasatch Fault only has to give an inch, or is it less? Anyway, whatever it is, it frightens me." Sarah stood waiting for the rushing sound that always followed the quaking tremors.

"Perhaps I'd better go to the house. I don't want the children to wake and not find me." If Sarah could have witnessed the actual explosion, the horrible results of the bomb just released, or its voraciousness in devouring the sleeping town, bringing about a complete annihilation, she would have seen that all her fears combined could not adequately bespeak the carnage wrought by such a bomb.

As the morning passed, Sarah's nerves tightened. Then she seemed to freeze as her worst fears came true in the excited voices of her children.

"Daddy, Daddy, look behind you, Daddy!" Young Jeremy dashed toward his father who was busy changing dams and intent on irrigating his ground. "Father, Father, look! This one is very low, just over St. George and is coming here! Do you see it,

Daddy?"

Jedediah Collins stopped, pulled a red bandana from the back pocket of his blue overalls, his squinting eyes glaring angrily at the oncoming cloud. "Yes, I see it, boy. We had better be heading for the house if we do not want a worried mother coming after us. Jeremy, you must always tend to what your mother says; I'm depending on you, boy."

Jenny came running from the grass-covered knoll where she and her five-year-old twin had been playing. "Isn't it pretty, Papa? So pink and so close! It isn't like the other clouds way up in the sky!"

Sarah, up at the house, had been listening to the radio all morning. This time the voice had instructed St. George residents to be on the alert as the nuclear cloud was definitely coming for them. The usual instructions were given to stay indoors for one hour. The deceptively smooth voice was sweetly modulated, *"Absolutely no danger — nothing to fear — but keep the children in. . . ,"* it repeated over and over.

Not stopping to turn off the radio, Sarah rushed from the house, wiping her hands on her apron as she ran. Seeing the cloud so low and almost directly over them, she froze. Suddenly, raising a trembling hand to her blanched face, an unsuspecting wail wrenched from her stiff lips. "Why us?" Running frantically toward her family, she nearly screamed, "Jed! Jeremy and Jenny! Come into the house immediately!"

"But it's so pretty, Mama." Little Jenny stood fascinated.

"Jed, please come." The near hysteria from his wife made him hurry.

"Come, children. I'll race you to the house," and they all dashed off.

The voice on the radio was again instructing people to go

indoors.

"Jed," Sarah's voice was shaky, "what about the cows, the horses, and the sheep? We take cover, but they graze out there." Her eyes moistened. "The feed, our garden — oh, Jed, it's so frustrating!"

"Honey, don't fret yourself. Our government knows what it's doing. . . ." He hesitated, "But I'd feel better if those clouds didn't come directly over us. Whatever fallout is, I don't want any part of it."

Sarah noticed the children's faces glued to the window pane, and forgetting the voice on the radio, she joined them.

"Look, Mama! The cloud is going a different color, and something shines in it!" Jenny stood enthralled.

"Just you be careful, Jenny. Sometimes pretty things can bite." Sarah hugged her small daughter.

"Like the gopher that bit Jeremy?" Jenny giggled.

"Worse than that, darling. And, please, stay in the house with mommy for a while." Sarah caught an occasional glitter drifting to earth, and as her eyes looked over their ground, she felt apprehensive. What would stop the deadly elements dropping to earth, and just how long would the ground be contaminated? she thought. In Sarah's heart she knew that the atoms were alive and would stay alive forever. She felt a wrench of foreboding, and nausea tore at her. Clutching the children hard, tears began coursing down her cheeks.

"Mama?" Fear and concern made the twins cry out. "Mama, what's the matter?"

"Oh, it's nothing, I guess. . . ," she tried to smile. "I — I guess it's just that I love you so much!"

The two hugged her hard and laughed, slightly relieved.

"We love you, too, Mama," they chorused.

Jed stood unobserved behind them, his face hard and as unreadable as a closed book. These three were his to hold, to protect, and to fend for. Today a new thought hit him hard. Perhaps, just perhaps, there was more to the fallout than one suspected. Confused, he stumbled into the kitchen.

Going to the sink, he stared, as one in a trance, then moved to watch the drifting atomic menace slowly move on toward other towns in its path. Jed's first fears were slowly being admitted; he felt the aftermath of the atomic bombs they frequently experienced could hold danger. He knew, too, the cloud was cooling and becoming smaller. Its color was changing into a sickly, purplish-pink with outer edges of pinkish-grey. He knew the neighboring towns on each side of St. George were equally contaminated depending upon the wind currents, though Newcastle and Enterprise were less populated.

Jed thought of his younger brother and family living in Newcastle five miles away. Concern for the health of this brother sent him hurrying from the house. Sarah became conscious of her husband's departure and ran to the kitchen door, flinging it wide.

"Jed, come back!" Sarah pleaded. "Please come back in!"

"Sarah, keep quiet. I'm going to St. George, then on to Newcastle. I'll keep the car windows up. You keep the twins in; they'll stay put with me away. And, Sarah, for their sakes and mine, you be careful." He looked haggard and tried to cover his emotions.

Back at the test site, men were working madly to gather the information they needed from the town that no longer existed.

CHAPTER 5

Brady Collins yawned, looking across the room at a picture placed prominently on the top shelf of his bookcase. Going to it, he flashed a crooked smile. "You know, there isn't another Sarah and Jed Collins in this old world like you, and that goes double for two high-spirited twins. Let's see. . . . " His nose crinkled, and his eyes grew misty. "I do believe you are past five now — yep, you were nearly four when I saw you last, a little over a year ago." Placing the picture back to its original position, he looked about the room, then started to undress.

Turning out the lights, he walked to the window and stood looking out upon the twinkling lights of Denver. A wave of homesickness caught him unaware, and he crumpled.

"Twenty-eight years old, Brady Collins, and tonight brought the cold truth to you that women are all alike, deceptive and cheating," he said out loud and sprawled upon the couch and debated his actions. "With or without a woman, that is the question," he groaned.

"I'll never find another Sarah, I guess. But it isn't a mother I want either. Just part of the qualities that come with her." He kicked his shoes off and retained only his boxer shorts and yawned drowsily. "Oh, well, can't win 'em all," he mumbled and fell asleep.

Brady jerked half consciously into life when something clanged into his awareness. Then half awake he muttered, "Drat — that phone. . . ." He groped about but found nothing. "It's down the hall, stup." Half asleep he fell, then crawled the remainder of the way, and in his sleepy awkwardness knocked it off the hook. Fumbling about, he finally retrieved it and yelled, "What the — talk to me? Oh, that's okay, I wasn't in bed. . . . No, honest. I *wasn't* in bed." He tried to laugh. "Sure I was reading. Who? Sure I know who you are," he said, wondering to himself who it really was. "Could I what?" Excitement stirred him. "When? Are you kidding? A transfer, huh? When do I have to be there? Two days?" Thrills raced over him. "Yes, sir — and if you need me quicker, I'll be at my folks' place in St. George, Utah. Thanks!"

Brady quick-stepped about the apartment humming "Home Sweet Home." Picking up the picture of his family again, a rumble escaped his lips, "See ya' tomorrow."

As morning broke, Brady lost no time in loading his duffle bag and calling his landlord. Giving a farewell salute, he walked jauntily from the apartment and climbed into his sports car. Manning the steering wheel, he quipped, "Let's be on our way, baby. We'll sure surprise 'um them time!"

The light of day was just beginning to fade as Brady Collins sped up the driveway to the rambling farmhouse on the outskirts of St. George. He held his breath as the nostalgia of many past years hit him.

"Why have I waited so long to come home?" Remorse was in his voice. "Even if Dad and I couldn't agree — surely — surely there is a way. . . ." The blowing of his horn had brought results, and as he stopped the car, out of the house rushed two rambunctious kids.

"Mom, it's Brady!" Brady caught the youngsters in his arms.

"Mama, Mama, it's Brady!" Jenny leaped onto his back, raining him with hugs and kisses.

"Hey, you two hoodlums, what's with all this mush?" he said, savoring all the attention until he noticed his mother. He gently removed his sister, and putting Jeremy aside, glided to his mother's side.

"Brady! Oh, Brady, you are home at last!" she sobbed with outstretched arms.

"Yep, I'm here, but only for a few hours," Brady grinned.

"A few hours?" Sarah looked at him, shocked. "Please, this time *try* to write, will you? Or at least telephone!" They walked into the house.

"This time I'll come in person. I'm being transferred to the test site near Las Vegas." He puffed out his chest. "Where's Pa?"

"Test site! Oh, Brady." Sarah looked away from her son. "Your father is tending to the chores." Walking to the kitchen sink, she tried to control her voice. "Brady, I'm worried about your father — he's working too hard; he's not well."

"Mom, why doesn't he sell out and take it easy? He could if he wanted to." Brady went to her side.

"Your father still cherishes the dream that you'll come back and work the farm with him." Sarah turned a beseeching look at him.

"Mom, remember what happened the last time we discussed this?" Brady took his mother by the shoulders and looked at her with compassion. "I'm sorry, Mom, but farming just isn't my bag. I'm a researcher. I love my job; right now I'm working for the government. We are involved in the atomic testing program. It's in my blood, Mom — I — I. . . ."

"Well, come on. I know you must be hungry." Sarah tried to smile, but before Brady could answer, the twins came rushing in and jumped on him. They went down, and Brady roughed them up.

"Jenny, Jeremy, you two go outside and let Brady eat in peace." Turning to him, she blinked back threatening tears. "They love you so much, Brady, and they miss you. Come eat. It's ready for you."

As Sarah and Brady turned toward the table, the door opened, and Jed, dusty and tired, came into the room. Brady looked sharply at his father. He's getting old, he thought. Father and son stood uncertain until Sarah's voice brought them together. "Aren't you two saying anything?"

"Hello, son. Glad to see you."

"Hello, Father. How are you?"

"Papa, our son has come to visit us; we are a family again." Sarah looked at her husband. "Come on in while Brady eats."

"Let the boy eat; I'll go shake this dust off and wash up a bit." Going to the kitchen sink, Jed washed his hands. "What brings you home this time, boy?"

"I got transferred to the test site near Vegas."

"Test site, hum?" Jed paused, then went on. "Good. Maybe you can get those boys to cut down on the dust they're kicking up. We have enough of our own without that nasty mess."

"Now, Pa. Remember I'm just a researcher."

"Well, you're so clever, maybe you could research a bomb that won't blow clouds over St. George." Jed looked at his son. "How long you going to be home this time?"

"Tonight and tomorrow maybe." Sarah began to clear up

the table. "Thought maybe we could go fishing. The old hole still there?" Brady laughed.

"No fishing."

"No fishing? What do you mean?" asked Brady, knowing that hole had always held the limit.

"There's just no fish." A bitter note touched the father's voice.

"Did the hole dry up?" Brady sounded puzzled.

"Fishing hole's still there — with plenty of water, too — just no fish." Jed looked hard at his son.

Sarah quickly intervened, "Since the fallout started and people began to wash their cars in the creek, a change has taken place in the stream."

"Can't understand all you're saying. Surely there isn't any danger," Brady said, perplexed.

"Another thing, Brady," his father said sternly, "if this testing continues, I'm afraid more than fish will die."

Brady looked at his father's retreating back.

"Mom, what you're implying — it couldn't be true."

Sarah Collins looked with compassion at her son and started to wash and put away the dishes. Brady feasted his eyes upon his mother. Her hair was no longer the raven black that curled about her pert, laughing face. It was streaked now with pure white, especially at the temples and above the ears. A swath of grey about an inch and a half at the center forehead revealed a wide widow's peak. The spontaneous smile was almost gone, but the laugh wrinkles were prominent. But it was the lack of color in her cheeks and the lost sparkle from her eyes, together with the stoop of her shoulders, that caught and held him most. "Why," he said to himself, "if she continues to shrink, I'll not have a mom."

"Mom, you're working too hard — so is dad; both of you have lost weight." Brady hugged her to him.

"Don't fret about us, Brady. Just you be my good son always." Sarah straightened to her usual five-foot five-inch stance. "Let's join your father in the living room. There's a special newscast about the tests on T.V." Brady took a seat behind his parents and watched them in silence. To his consternation, his father was hardly the man he used to know. There was a stoop to his shoulders and a perpetual hack on his lips. His now dogged look of do or die upon a once jovial face was harsh. His six foot height, which Brady had inherited, seemed to have withered slightly. The mop of sandy hair, also a gift to Brady, was thinning, and the face was eroding away.

Brady felt suddenly cheated; his years away could never be replaced. Affectionately, his dad's arm drew his mother close, and he heard a quiver in the dying timber of his father's voice.

"Woman, as long as I have you. . . ."

Brady suddenly felt more left out than ever and was glad when the T.V. interrupted his thoughts.

"The support of the people in Southern Utah, Nevada, and part of Arizona is to be commended," came the mellow voice of the Salt Lake newscaster. "The personnel at the test site and the government are exerting every effort and expending all avenues to assure the safety of the area." He continued, "They reaffirm there is no danger in any way."

"Mom, Dad, this should make you real proud to be among those praised." Brady received no comment, and knowing he was ignored, tried again. "Dad, why are you and Mom so hostile about these tests?"

Jed arose, pulling his wife with him. He turned, almost savagely upon his son.

33

"You go do your work Brady, the job you love. Just remember this: those downwinds that carry the non-existing dangers to us may cause you more hurt than you bargained for. If they are so harmless, Brady, why be so picky in not letting them hit the big cities like Las Vegas or Los Angeles? Tell me that, Brady?" Jedediah started for the bedroom but quickly turned around. "I was gullible once, too, son, but not anymore. Some maniac is running us over, and to him a few thousand lives means nothing. No, Brady, those beautiful man-made clouds, that fascinate most, cannot help but drop deadly matter."

Brady fell silent as he looked at the clock and was shocked to see the hands at ten-thirty.

"Good night, Dad — Mom." He was a little disturbed and stretched out full length upon the floor, content to listen to the lulling voice of assurance coming from the T.V.

CHAPTER 6

"Brady. Brady, dear. Wake up, son. You need your rest, and I'm sure your bed will feel better than the floor." Sarah shook her son gently.

"Mom," Brady opened his eyes and blinked at his mother. "Umm, Mom, I forgot to turn off the T.V. I'm sorry."

"It's all right, son. Please go to bed."

"I'll bet the T.V. woke you." Brady looked at the time. "One-thirty? Whew! I'm tired, I guess."

"No, Brady. The T.V. didn't disturb me. It's your father. He's finding it rough to sleep nights. I have to see that he gets his pain pill."

"Is Dad that bad?" Brady hesitated. "My coming home hasn't done him any good either. I think I'll take off early in the morning. I do love my job, Mom. I hope at least you understand."

"Brady, I do understand. I know your father is a born farmer. You, Brady, are his double physically, but you have always wanted to research things out." Sarah looked with admiration at him. "I'm proud of you, Brady; I would have talked you into staying once but not now."

Brady got to his feet, and taking his mother by the shoulders, looked into her eyes and spoke urgently.

"Mom, you know I irritate Dad; I'm just not the son he wanted." Brady looked depressed.

"Son, your father is very proud of you. . . ." There was a catch in her voice. "You should hear him brag about you, but he works too hard and is worried about your Uncle Dale."

"I know he works too hard. Why don't you sell and move into St. George?"

"Why, Brady! Your dad would fold completely if he couldn't have his land and his animals." Sarah shivered. "No, Brady. You couldn't ask that of him."

"Mom, I can't tell him goodbye. I love all of you too much to hurt you. Will you please tell him goodbye for me?" Brady turned from her. "I love him so much it hurts me to have to hurt him."

Jed lay tautly in his bed listening intently to their voices as tears slid unconsciously from his eyes.

"I'll tell him, Brady, but I'm sure he knows." Sarah kissed her son. "Come to bed, Brady, and don't worry about your father. He loves you."

"Sarah, you know your man better than he does himself," Jedediah silently muttered to himself. "The world may go astray, but as long as I have you, things will be all right." He feigned sleep as Sarah came to the bed.

"Love, are you awake?" came her voice gently. "I have your pill."

"Huh — oh, is it you, Sarah?" Jed sat up. "Come to bed." His voice was husky. "Needn't fuss so over an old man."

"Old man!" Sarah's voice was full of emotion. "Jedediah Collins, you're the best man alive. Just you never forget it."

A chuckle came from him, and as the warmth of her body nestled up to him, his fears vanished.

The next morning a peaceful feeling filled the atmosphere about the Collins acres and especially permeated in the big house so immaculately kept by Sarah. And as the five-year-old twins came into the kitchen struggling with Brady's duffle bag, they made a gleeful sight for everyone. Going to them, Brady picked each up under an arm along with the bag. As they kicked and squealed, Brady walked across the big porch and down the steps to the car and dumped them both into the back seat.

"Guess I'll take you with me," he teased.

Sarah followed them to the porch, laughing. It was good to have the pranks of Brady back again. This son was equaled by none and born with the flush of an overwhelming new love and eager youth. Jed had captured her heart at eighteen, and Brady was born while she was but nineteen. The twins were born surprisingly at the close of her child bearing years after all hopes of a family had passed. The love for these children was different somehow. They brought new hope and the solid assurance that love never grows old.

The twins hopped out of the car and rushed to their mother. Little Jenny still clung to Brady's cap which she had hardly taken from her head since she first stole it at his arrival. Taking his mother into his arms, he kissed her hard.

"Take care of yourself, Mom, and Dad, too. Tell him goodbye for me." Taking his cap from the flaxen-haired girl, he chuckled, "And you, you little rascal, take care of Dad and Mom." Brady walked quickly to his car and sped away, too emotional to look back.

As Brady drew up at the checking station, giving him entrance to the test site, a uniformed guard came out and stood in front of his car, then walked to his door.

"May I help you, sir?" the guard asked.

"Yes, I believe you can." Brady handed the guard his pass. The guard took it and walked into the checkpost and picked up the phone. Brady, impatient to be off, tapped his fingers nervously upon the steering wheel. He turned the radio louder and tried to sing along with the song, his eyes upon the guard.

"Thank you, sir, for being patient, but these things take time. You are to report to General Freeman. He is waiting for you. Just follow the signs to Area Five; you can't get lost."

"Thank you." Brady drove away, joining in on the song on his radio.

A moment later Brady drew up at the main complex, and snatching his attache case, approached another guard and asked brusquely, "General Freeman, if you will, please."

"Yes, sir," the guard saluted. "Down the hall, sir, to your right. It's the first door. You can't miss the nameplate, sir."

"You always stand that way?" Brady joked with a large grin.

"Yes, sir!" The guard stood erect.

"What a way to make a living." Brady started down the hall, then turned, nodding at the guard. "Relax, soldier, and don't vanish. I may need you again."

Brady felt some apprehension as he read the bold lettering upon the door. "General George Freeman must be pretty high on himself to demand recognition like this, especially at Mercury," he thought outloud. Carefully, Brady rapped on the door.

"Come in," a smooth voice commanded.

Brady straightened himself and opened the door and walked in.

38

"Well, Collins, we didn't expect you till tomorrow," said the general, glancing up from his desk. A smirk crossed his almost smooth face as he pointed at a chair. "Sit down."

"Dedication, sir. It's a habit of mine," Brady said and dropped into the chair. As he made himself comfortable, he became aware of Freeman's eyes upon him.

"You, ah. . . ," the general cleared his throat, "drive a sports car?"

"You must have spies, General. Sorry, sir. I'm not too militarily oriented." Brady removed his cap.

"All right, Collins. And now, let's get down to business." Freeman expanded his chest imposingly. "You are a very lucky man."

"How's that, sir? I've been told all research is important." Brady knew his profession well.

The general felt the iron in Brady's words and instantly become cautious. Without turning to Brady, Freeman looked out the window and spoke again.

"Collins, the most important thing a young man — any man for that matter — can do is to be involved in the defense of his country."

Brady wondered what was coming next. He nonchalantly picked up an expensive pen from Freeman's desk while waiting to find out. As he examined it, the cartridge shot across the room, so he quickly dropped the pen back on the desk before the general turned around.

"Whether one is a soldier in the field or a worker in the government in defense of his country — it makes little difference. I commend you for your interest and dedication and hope our nuclear testing comes first with you. We need dedicated men like you here. Your distinction as a scientist brought you here. I hope your work keeps you here." Freeman stepped across the room to a filing cabinet, and after removing some papers, returned to his seat behind the desk. "You have been cleared, and we know that you are single, conscientious, dependable, and almost obnoxiously honest."

"Your spies again, sir?" mused Brady.

The slyly smiling face of the general irritated Brady. Freeman's expression had hardly changed since he entered the room.

"We demanded that you be here," Freeman went on. "You have been assigned to work with one, Doctor Charity Fuller." Freeman's grin became lopsided. "Oh, she is very competent in all aspects, as a doctor of science and. . . ." he cut himself short. "I think you'll find her quite refreshingly different from your other co-workers."

Freeman looked at Brady, and the cold steel in his eyes made Brady take a deeper look at the man before him.

"Collins, Doctor Fuller is an A-1 scientist, and her work is very outstanding. But. . . ." Freeman's fingers rapped hard upon his desk, "her irrationality and her outspokenness on matters that should not concern her can be, shall we say, trying."

Brady felt the hair rising on his neck and a dislike for Freeman starting to grow.

"Collins, I'm telling you ahead of time so you won't be distracted by her opinions and politics. See if you can curb the woman and still be amicable." Freeman's blue-white eyes bore into Brady. "Do I make myself clear, Collins?"

"Yes, sir! Perfectly clear," and before he could say more, a knock came upon Freeman's door.

"Come in!" The command was harsh. "What is it?"

"Sorry to bother you, General, but these papers need to be

signed." The messenger sheepishly placed the papers on Freeman's desk and waited.

Freeman picked up the pen Brady had made useless. And, as the general struggled with it, Brady smiled to himself. Irritation showed upon Freeman's face when the pen didn't write. Looking at Brady, he gritted, "Well, Collins, I've enjoyed our visit here. You may go now." Freeman threw the pen across the room. "I'm looking forward to your being here."

"Thank you, sir." Brady took his time in getting up. Then, with deliberate provocation, he reached into his pocket and handed the general his own pen. The messenger's face showed amusement, and Freeman's face was getting more florid by the minute.

"Thanks, Collins. That pen is worthless." As Freeman took the pen, Brady rocked back and forth on his heels, immensely enjoying the situation. General Freeman sensed the loss of face before the estimable Collins and barked a dismissal to the messenger.

"Thank you, sir!" The messenger vanished, and Brady also walked toward the door. He paused, then turned with a snappy salute to the general and exited briskly into the hall, just in time to collide with a head-bent female studiously assessing some papers. With a jolt the woman came erect and glared at the beaming Brady, who was now standing in a shower of paper.

Doctor Charity Fuller started to open her mouth, then clamped her jaws hard, her eyes hard rays of disbelief and concern. Brady, in an instant, assessed each point of the woman before him and passed her on all points.

"Whew, pennies from heaven," a glitter of admiration brought his face alive. "Let me get these papers, please."

"No! Just leave things as they are," Charity barked. "I'll

41

need to put them in order again." Charity's face was glowing pink from Brady's open admiration. Her dark auburn hair looked redder than usual, and her lips trembled slightly. "I — I can do this better myself; they will have to go back in order."

"I'm just trying to help; you see, providence did put you in the path." Brady's face was dead pan. "You cannot thwart the inevitable; and I caused the upheaval, so I'm the accountable one. Besides, I'm just trying to help."

"I'm sure, then, if you want to help so desperately, the janitor will give you a job." Charity Fuller's look dripped ice as she gathered up the papers, then tried to take from Brady's hands what he had gathered. "If you don't mind, I'll take these."

"Pretty please?" Brady stepped back, rocking slightly upon his toes, devilment gleaming upon his face. Charity stood militarily erect, her face frozen. "Sir, if you please, I'd like my papers back and thank you." Retrieving her papers, she turned and nearly clicking her heels, walked from him.

As Charity went into her office and closed the door, Brady picked up his attache case and walked out into the bright sunlight. Going to his car, he took out his duffle bag and hesitated. Then putting it back inside, he stretched, yawned, then leaned against the car, one foot on the fender. His eyes took in what he could see of the test site, and he found himself really wondering what it was all about. A loneliness — or tinge of something foreign to his senses — tugged at him.

"Come on, Collins, you're on the soil of the good old U.S.A. Can't let the jitters throw you now," he reassured himself. Taking his bag up again, he sauntered back into the building and asked for Doctor Charity Fuller's office. Brady found the nameplate as directed and knocked upon the door, and receiving no answer, opened the door and walked in.

Tipping his cap back upon his head, he whistled softly at the faint but provocative reminder that a female worked here. Brady sniffed and smiled, then walked about investigating.

"Too bad the red-headed angel couldn't be the Dr. Fuller. Yeah, just my luck to be panned off on some Amazon skirt of fifty years," said Brady finding himself alone. He raised his eyes mockingly and threw himself on a couch that was partly secluded from the main office. Thirty minutes went by, and still he was alone except for the recent memory of the red-head he had bumped into. Kicking off his shoes and making himself comfortable, he settled down to wait.

CHAPTER 7

Charity Fuller dashed into her office at quitting time, locked the desk drawers, picked up her purse, then left, locking the door behind her, never seeing the sleeping Brady. "One more day. . . ." her eyes sparkled. "I wonder just where Freeman will put his new stooge this time. This one could be very clever." She shrugged her shoulders. "Oh, well, it takes all kinds to make a world." That night Charity drove into Las Vegas and picking up her girlfriend who worked at the Reynolds Electric Company, a company attached to the test site, let herself unwind with some night life.

It was early morning the following day as Charity drove down the Tonopah Highway, alert to her surroundings. As always, the scenes of the desert thrilled her, with its vast unknown life. Yet she had seen it ablaze with a myriad of soft, bewitching colors in early spring. Strange, she thought, how things can be so different from what they seem.

Only too quickly she was back at Mercury, and the day awaited her. Early as usual, she hummed a light tune and inadvertently caught herself thinking of the man she had run into the day before. Opening her office door and shutting it quickly, she walked toward the corner made into her private retreat. Charity saw the shoes on the floor first and stiffled a squeal. Then, cautiously, she stepped to the sofa and came erect instantly.

"Not you!" she screamed, her hand going to her mouth. "It can't be you!" she quivered with a stiffled sob as her purse fell to the floor.

Slowly Brady opened his blurry eyes. As they encountered the shocked face of the bright-eyed young woman above him, he shut them hard and covered them with both hands, then opened them again, slowly looking at her from between his fingers. A lazy smile tweaked his lips and with a groan he rolled to the floor.

"Good morning!" Brady got to his feet and rubbed the back of his neck. He grimaced as he stretched. "Bad bed — but worth the awakening."

"What are you doing in here and how did you get in?" The angrier she got the more beautiful she became, thought Brady.

"Good morning again. Still a glorious day." Brady grinned her down.

"Well, I guess it's a good morning to you, whoever you are, but — but. . . ."

"That's better," Brady gazed at her bent head. "First I'm here to work with a Doctor Charity Fuller. We are to be partners in researching some aspects of the atomic bomb. Second, let me introduce myself. I'm Brady Collins, male, twenty-eight years old, and, by the way," his grin spread quickly over his countenance, "I'm single."

Charity swallowed, walked to the window, and looked out, her equilibrium taking time to adjust. "It is a good morning, Mr. Collins. And, yes, I do know why you are here. Now if you would please tell me how you got into this office, I'd be grateful."

"Are you Doctor Charity Fuller?" Brady croaked. Then he laughed aloud. "Of all the sneaky quirks I've been thrown, this beats them all." Rubbing his hands together, he gloated, "Pleased to meet you, Doctor Charity. I'm glad I came here." Walking to her side, he spoke playfully, "I was told to come to your office by General Freeman and, to be explicit, to wait for you. Then I was supposed to get my orders." He shot her a guarded look. "This I did and apparently was asleep on the couch when you locked me in." Seeing her discomfiture, he walked to his duffle bag and started to leave the room. "I wonder if you could tell me where to go to shower? I'd like to shave and clean up a bit."

"Oh," Charity blushed as she turned to him, "I'm sorry about last night. It — it was a terrible oversight, Mr. Collins. I hope you don't expect more than my apology. You do have that. Now, I have work to do."

"Guess you wouldn't extend your apology to scrubbing my back?" Brady saw the anger rush into her eyes. "No? Well, I didn't think so."

As the door closed behind him, Charity covered her face with her hands and sank upon a chair, too stunned yet to think coherently.

Brady shaved, showered, and somewhat refreshed soon found food to appease his hunger. After eating, he quietly relaxed in the employees' lounge.

"Mr. Collins?" Charity spoke from behind him in a stilted tone. "General Freeman has instructed me to take you on a tour of the area and to acquaint you with your responsibilities as soon as you are free. I'll be in my office." Charity turned to go.

"But I'm ready now, Doctor. No use wasting time." He got to his feet and smirked. "Should I salute you, Doctor? Since my arrival here, I've heard nothing but mister and sir, general and doctor. I'm wondering just how to address you." He shot a sharp glance at her. "I wish you'd call me Brady."

"If it makes you feel better, I'll call you Brady. As far as the others. . . ."

"What should I call you?" Brady cut her short.

"Just call me Doctor Fuller. Our work will be together but. . . ."

"But outside of work it's to be hands off." Brady finished for her. "That's quite all right with me, Doctor. You did say a tour of the grounds, huh? Bombs away." Brady followed the stiff-backed woman as she hurried away.

As they sped along, Brady was amazed at the vastness of what he saw. Little knolls, dry lake beds, more lake beds, and it went on and on.

"This is where the next shot is to be set up," said Charity, pointing to a designated spot.

"Why so far out?" Brady frowned.

"Concussion, of course. And shock waves." Fuller looked hard at him. "You've come here to learn, Brady, and you'll get more than you want."

"You mean atmospheric shock waves?" His look questioned her.

"Basically. If ground zero were any closer to the base, the shock waves alone would destroy most everything standing."

"I knew there would be shock waves, but I never imagined them to be that powerful," Brady admitted and frowned harder.

"You'll never know just how powerful until you've experienced it for yourself. In fact," Charity went on, "the reverse shock, that is, backlash of the explosion when the vacuum at ground zero is replaced, is every bit as strong as the

47

initial blast that hits you." Fuller was obviously knowledgeable Brady conceded to himself, and as they parked the jeep and walked through the monitoring area, they came to a control point.

"Here we measure the strength and various effects of the shots," instructed Charity. "Obviously, each test has specific purposes, and the data is recorded as collected by these instruments. For instance, maybe we want to measure the effects of a large detonation on ground mass. When the device goes off, it does the same thing to the ground around it that a large rock does to a quiet pond when the rock hits the water."

"Rippling?" Brady responded.

"Large ripples. I'd say waves." Charity looked at Brady. "The shock waves rumble St. George and other towns, too. The swish of the atmospheric pressure precedes the shake, and then the cloud dispersion follows the prevailing winds in their usual patterns away from Las Vegas and Los Angeles."

"Incredible," was all that Brady could muster.

As they looked through the glass at the observation tower, Charity gestured, "From here you are able to see the entire operation. As you can see, it takes hundreds of people and millions of dollars to run this project. Engineers, scientists, carpenters, electricians, you name it, we've got it." There was a hard note in her voice. They stood close, looking at the activity and bustling below them.

"And General Freeman? How does he fit into the picture?" Brady looked the woman straight in the eyes.

"I think you've seen everything. Shall we go?" responded Charity, ignoring the question.

As Charity turned, Brady lingered and took in the scene below. His brow was creased, and the unwillingness of Charity to talk about Freeman slightly irritated him. Finally he joined her at the jeep, and they rode back in complete silence.

As the two walked into her office, Brady shut the door with a purposeful click and walked to the window, looking out. After several minutes, he turned to face Fuller.

"I told you, Brady. I don't want to talk about it," Charity shot out, anticipating Brady's question.

"I get the impression somehow that you don't like General Freeman?" Brady smirked.

"You're not listening, Collins. I said I don't want to talk about it." She drew herself to her full height.

"Ah, Doctor Fuller, I don't mean to pry, but. . . ."

"Then don't! We'll get along just fine if you do your job and let me do mine." Charity was white with anger. Brady stood looking at the woman and sensed she should be alone.

"You're the boss, Doctor. I'm just here to help." He walked out into the fresh air, his thoughts quite erratic. Taking a deep breath he soliloquized, "There has to be an answer to every question. It will come, man. Just be patient."

CHAPTER 8

As Brady Collins dug deeper into his job, the many facets of his new work awoke latent powers his old job had dulled. This was exciting to him. The pulverized ground, the complete demolition of everything in a certain radius, the force of destruction, the traveling time of sound, its wind force and the length of time a bomb cloud drifted before its extinction, clothes contamination, the colors best for conductive purposes, water pollution, radiation effects upon vegetation and animals in outlying districts; the list of new experiences was endless.

Brady knew understanding these things was essential in a nuclear war, especially for America. And he felt deeply the need to know every answer to every question so Americans could better defend themselves in an atomic war. Yet, the deeper he explored into the causes and effects, the more awesome the answers came chilling to his mind concerning just how much death was in a bomb of such magnitude.

Brady was a constant questioner of all workers at the site: electricians, carpenters, engineers; he wanted to know every detail. His work with Doctor Fuller was exciting. But in the back of his head the connection between cancer and radiation they had discovered scared him.

Neither Brady nor Fuller challenged the other in any way, but each worked together amicably during the days and went a separate way at night, even though their apartments were not far apart.

After each bomb release, the powers that made the wheels turn met in conference to digest, dissect, compare, and analyze every angle. The atomic bomb had to be under safe control and not become a deadly toy of the ruthless.

This day the consultation room was filled to capacity. Blackboards were full of diagrams and nuclear vocabulary with the instructor driving into the minds of those present the reality of all that was taking place. People were busy taking notes as they listened.

General Freeman sat, like a crowned king, at the head of the table while Brady and Dr. Fuller faced each other across the table as other personnel, both military and civilian, occupied the remaining seats.

Brady looked at Charity and knew she was strung high for some cause. He tried to catch her eye, but she deliberately ignored his look. Catching Freeman's eyes upon her too, a wave of dislike for the man tore through him. Brady had seen that look before — calculating and destructive. Brady intercepted Freeman's stare, and the general gave a satisfied smirk as he nodded at Collins.

"Eyes of ice," Brady breathed under his breath. "Cold, calculating, cutting, and deadly. He's a devil in disguise." Looking again at Charity, he sensed her vulnerability and felt fear trickle into his bloodstream. "Better be on your guard, Collins; things ain't what they ought to be here," mused Brady.

After the instructor had ended his lecture, Freeman arose,

frowning self-importantly, his stature radiating command. "Are there any questions?"

"General. . . ," Charity rolled her pencil through her fingers, not looking at Freeman.

"Dr. Fuller," General Freeman waved an airy dismissal at her, "I'll speak with you later." His eyes looked away from her. "These people must get back to work."

Brady watched the drama before him and knew Freeman was putting her off intentionally, reducing her to almost nothing. When the meeting ended, Brady got to his feet and leisurely sauntered out the door, and as Charity remained alone with Freeman, he leaned nonchalantly against the wall just outside, listening intently to them.

"Well, Fuller, what is it this time?" Freeman's voice was nasty.

"We just received reports of illness in the town of Alamo. Dr. Phillips brought back reports that all radiation levels, especially those in Alamo, were much higher than had been previously anticipated." Charity's voice registered fear.

"Did Dr. Phillips tell the people in Alamo that the radiation was that high?" Freeman's voice was sharp and harsh.

"Yes, he did. But that's not the point, General, and you know it, too. If the people in Alamo are feeling the effects of what is probably radiation sickness, the people in St. George are in serious trouble also."

At the mention of St. George, Brady's ears picked up, and he leaned more intently toward the door, more disturbed than he dared admit. Suddenly the faces of his father and mother came before him, and he again heard the fears they had uttered; lost energy, haggard faces, it all began to make sense. What did it mean? Freeman's voice came out to him clear and sharp.

"Fuller, I order you to keep your mouth shut about this." Freeman had walked to the window and now turned, angered beyond control. "I'm sure there is a reasonable explanation for this. Phillips had no authority." He almost choked with heat. "He had no right to let out this information without my sanction." He walked to his desk, hitting it hard. "I'm in command here!"

"Command or no command," Charity stood her ground defiantly, never raising her voice but emphasizing each word, "you let this go without some investigation and you are in dire trouble. If the news media gets this report, you'll have a lot of explaining to do," she threatened.

"Why you. . . ." Freeman choked. "How dare you even intimate my duty to me! I'll — I'll. . . ."

"You'll what, Freeman? You know I have enough information to blacken you before the entire world." Dr. Charity Fuller looked with loathing eyes at the raging general, picked up her papers, and walked briskly from the room, nearly colliding with Brady in the hallway.

"Doctor, I heard what you said about St. George. My folks live there," Brady said, taking her arm and stopping her. "Is there really any danger? Maybe Freeman is right," Brady remarked. "Perhaps there isn't anything to worry about."

"Collins, wake up! Freeman is a freedom fighter — he's fighting a cold war, and nothing, not anyone, matters to him but blowing up desert." Charity looked at Brady with pity and compassion. "Your people happen to be among the innocent, the unsuspecting. Brady, I'm sorry."

"But, Doctor Fuller, we're in the middle of nowhere out here, and St. George, Alamo, and those other small towns around here surely couldn't be contaminated," Brady pleaded

53

for assurance.

"Brady, you've been here for two test shots now. Surely you noticed the winds had to be blowing in the direction of St. George before we let a detonation off. And remember the one test scheduled for last Thursday when a half-hour before zero the winds changed towards Las Vegas, and instantly Freeman was like a madman until he had cancelled the test? If you remember we were on meathooks for two days, and Freeman was a wildman before the winds changed, and the bomb was finally exploded."

"But Freeman insists the tests show that the radiation is dispersed before it hits St. George and that the cloud is harmless even before it hits them," Brady's voice cracked with emotion and hope.

"Brady, use your scientific brain and not your heart. You can't remove the danger simply because you will it." Charity placed her hand on his arm, then walked away.

An hour later the phone shrilled through Charity's office, and she spoke briskly as she picked it up. "Fuller speaking! Yes, Mildred — he's here." Turning to Brady she smiled, giving him the phone. "It's for you. It's your mother."

"Hello, Mom! No, you didn't interrupt anything important." Brady sensed trouble. "Mom? What's the matter? Oh, no! When? Yes, I'll be there immediately. Sure I can come. Goodbye, Mom." Brady slowly hung up the phone and stood in a slump for a few minutes before he turned to face Charity.

"Is there something wrong?"

"My uncle died this morning; he was only fifty-five, and Mom was wondering if I could possibly come home."

"Oh, Brady, I'm so terribly sorry," Charity consoled. "Of course, you can go home."

"Will you miss me for a couple of days?" They looked at

each other as if it were for the first time, then Brady gave a smile. "Now that's a corny question." For the first time they really laughed together.

"It's okay, Brady. You go ahead." She hesitated, then said, "I'm willing to bet that you'll find out your uncle died of cancer or leukemia."

"Charity," her name came easily to his lips, "I knew you would think it's because of radiation from the tests."

Charity turned from him before she spoke. "Let me put it this way. I wouldn't drink any milk while I was in St. George if I were you."

"You really are suspicious, aren't you?" Brady's knees nearly let him down.

"I have many reasons to be, Brady." She raised her head, her eyes on his.

"Well, I guess we'll face the consequences now, one way or the other." He looked differently at the woman before him. "I'd hate to think Uncle Dale has sold us short, though."

"Brady, remember this: Freeman isn't the U.S.A., and these so-called freedom fighters will have much to answer for. Get going; you're needed at home."

CHAPTER 9

$\mathbf{A}$fter General Freeman's encounter at the meeting with Charity, he walked to the telephone and nearly fell into the closest chair. Rapping his knuckles nervously on the desk, he picked up the phone and dialed. Impatiently, he waited for an answer to the ring.

"Mayfield, I want my car ready to leave for Alamo immediately. And, Mayfield, put the *bigger* flag on the car today. Yes, yes, and Dr. Phillips will be going with us today." Freeman smiled indulgently.

As Brady squealed to a stop at the checking station on his way to St. George, he nearly bumped into the rear of a big limousine ahead of him. Removing his cap, he scratched his head. Perplexity made him scowl. "Well, well, I do believe that's Freeman."

The guard heard his remark and smiled. "Sure is and is he ever decked out. I couldn't help but see all those medals."

"Why is the car flag so prominent today?" Brady quizzed.

"Dunno, but they're going to Alamo." The guard was informative.

"They? Wasn't he alone?" Brady grinned.

"Not today. Dr. Phillips was with him, and Freeman was chewing at the bit." The guard checked him out.

"Be seeing you," Brady waved and shot forward. "Freeman and Phillips going to Alamo — and Freeman waving Old Glory. I wonder — ?" Brady turned on the radio and scowled heavily as his thoughts raced.

"Sir," Mayfield addressed the general, "that's Collins right behind us, and he's in one big hurry."

General Freeman raised an eyebrow and smirked, "Nothing to worry about there, Mayfield." Freeman shot an indulgent glance at the man beside him. "Phillips, sometimes people get too big for their britches."

Doctor Hugh Phillips looked at the general and frowned, not knowing quite what to make of the general's statement.

"Take Doctor Charity Fuller. Too smart in her assumptions and too eager to speak what she thinks. Now take Collins," a gloating leer curled his lips, and the clipped, well-groomed mustache twitched, "I have him going my way, and Fuller is having a hard time leading him her way." A metallic glitter shot from his eyes.

Phillips sensed an antagonistic meaning behind the general's words, and an uneasiness began to gnaw inside him. What was the significance of this hurried trip and what induced the general to dress so regally today? These questions occurred to the doctor, but he knew the man beside him well enough to keep quiet.

Mayfield, acting as chauffeur, continued to drive into Vegas. "The usual place," said Freeman relaxed as they reached the edge of town.

Mayfield manipulated the gleaming black Cadillac and

came to a smooth stop in the curved driveway of a spacious house guarded by iron gates. The chauffeur quickly ejected himself from the front seat and with a smart salute immediately opened the door for the general, who motioned for Phillips to remain seated.

Puzzled, Doctor Phillips looked at Mayfield, and as their eyes met, a knowing wink and a smothered smile came from the driver.

Moments later, the general emerged, and Doctor Phillips caught his breath as he gazed upon the woman decorating Freeman's arm. To Phillips it was as if Venus herself stood before him.

"Phillips," the lash in Freeman's voice brought Phillips down to earth, "I'd appreciate you taking the front seat. On your way, Mayfield," Freeman barked, looking straight ahead. "And waste no time."

"Yes, sir!" Mayfield slammed the door behind the general and scampered to his seat.

As the miles slipped by and the road to Alamo became obvious, Doctor Phillips felt a resentment gnaw in his innards. "Mayfield, we're going to Alamo today?" Phillips asked.

"Yes, sir," replied the driver. "General's orders." The soldier shot Phillips a sardonic look. "Hot business there I hear," he added with a sneer.

Shifting slightly, the doctor felt restless. "Just what is Freeman up to anyway?" he mumbled to himself.

As the car sped up the mountainous road leading into Alamo, the general's clipped voice ordered Mayfield to drive to the town hall. As they drew up to the building, Freeman's voice was cool. "A welcoming committee I see. Oh, it's just as well."

Mayfield swerved the car to the curb and opened the door

for the general before sauntering to Phillips and with a mocking smile opened his door. General George Freeman, resplendent in dress uniform, medals gleaming, boldly stepped from the car and indicated for Phillips to do likewise.

"I'm Burton Jennings. I kind of act as mayor around here," said a red-cheeked rotund man who extended his hand in greeting. "Dr. Phillips said he would get help for us, but we didn't expect it would come so soon and from the top brass," Jennings beamed.

"Jennings, I'm General George Freeman; of course, you know Doctor Phillips." Freeman's chest expanded, his smile grew facetious. "It's because of Doctor Phillips that we are here." His eyes roved over the crowd, whittling them down to peasants. "And I'm here with good news instead of bad."

"I don't know what you mean," Jennings broke in. "We all now Doctor Phillips was honest with us. We are in danger, aren't we?"

"Nonsense! I'm here to correct this fallacy and to assure you again that there is no danger. This area has little, if any, radiation at all. You can be assured we have your welfare at heart. It's such people as you that make this great nation what it is." Freeman's velvety voice soothed the fiery Jennings, and he flashed his ready smile to the crowd.

"But, General, the reports I submitted. . . ." Phillips interjected, stepping forward.

"Doctor, a miscalculation." Freeman interrupted.

"What about everyone being sick?" stammered Jennings, his voice now full of heat.

"Who knows? Coal dust, flu, bad food. Could be a number of things. The government cannot be liable for all ailments." The general's authoritative voice hushed the murmuring crowd.

"Well, it was very nice meeting all of you. Call upon us anytime, mayor."

Phillips turned to the crowd, looking bewildered and shouted, "I'll get to the bottom of this. I assure you."

The general only glared at him.

"Thank you, Dr. Phillips." A look of appreciation went to the doctor from Jennings, then he turned accusingly to Freeman. "*As* the *General* is dealing the cards, we won't hold our breath. But, we know now how the winds are blowing, and for now it is as the general directs."

"Coming, Phillips?" Freeman shouted. "No time to waste here. I want to go to St. George."

Mayfield stood beaming, thinking the general had outwitted everyone. After ten years of chauffeuring Freeman around, he had picked up some of the ways of his boss. The two understood each other perfectly.

As the general settled himself beside the woman, his hand caressed her flawless bare arm, then slid possessively about her shoulders, drawing her to him.

"Lisha, my lovely Lisha, I'm sorry to expose you to such degradation, but it's all in a day's work." Conceit flashed in his pale eyes and brought a self-indulgent smile.

Doctor Phillips took his seat beside the chauffeur and smiled at the new image he had formed of Freeman and Mayfield. "How wrong can a man be?" he shuttered. His soliloquy was meant for himself, but Mayfield's voice jolted him to awareness.

"About what, Doctor?"

"Things in general," Phillips responded awkwardly. "I've learned never to expect too much from people — set rules aren't for all."

"Yah, it's great to have power over life, isn't it, Doctor?" Mayfield was rambling, but Phillips read the hidden meaning in Mayfield's words.

"Well, that depends." Hugh Phillips' smile was a little sardonic.

"Depends on what, Doctor?" Mayfield asked inquisitively.

"Whether man uses this power to destroy or save lives." Hugh's blue eyes shown like the mountain sky as he wondered just how deep Mayfield would get. "Mayfield," Hugh's voice was harsh, "there is a law of recompense meted to each man, be it harsh or gentle. . . ."

"Oh, Doctor. Man makes his own destiny. I've seen it work for years," Mayfield gloated.

Hugh Phillips hated to be interrupted and turned to the chauffeur, his eyes sparking fire. "Mayfield, even the general will someday get his. No man can play God and not pay."

"You don't know our general." Mayfield threw back his head and laughed.

Because of the glass shield between them and being too intent on other things, Freeman heard nothing of the conversation in the front seat. As they sped over the miles, Doctor Phillips drew himself into his thoughts about the people in Alamo. It all started to jell now, and the blatant untruths Freeman was propogating riled him. He now knew Freeman to be beneath respectability. He also perceived the unquenchable force driving the general to accomplish what he was doing regardless of cost or hazard, and it frightened him.

As they drove into St. George, Freeman barked orders to drive about town. The gleaming chauffeur-driven limousine, the decorated, smiling general, and the flag waving from each front fender made quite a spectacle.

Suddenly, Hugh Phillips recognized Brady Collins standing on the sidewalk and was about to call to him when he disappeared in the crowd. The look of hostility that had been on Collins' face made Phillips clamp his mouth shut. Thinking perhaps either Freeman or Mayfield had seen Brady, too, he waited for their acknowledgment. As none came, he sighed audibly.

"Quite a day for you, eh, Doctor? Perhaps even a new experience," Mayfield prodded, the ridicule in his voice was clearly intended.

"Each dog has his day," Phillips spoke through gritted teeth. "Each dog has his day."

CHAPTER 10

Brady's thoughts lingered upon the general, and knowing Dr. Phillips was with him added a frown to his face. "I wonder what the general is up to?" Brady asked himself aloud. "Charity was upset about Alamo and its people — I'm curious — and now what's Phillips part in all this?" Mechanically, Brady leaned into his car and switched on the radio. As a romantic tune filled the air, the face of Charity Fuller came before him.

"Screwball!" He laughed aloud. Brady Collins, twenty-eight years old and asking a woman like Charity Fuller if she'd miss him.

A grease-stained gas attendant in shabby overalls two sizes too big for him abruptly jerked Brady back to reality.

"Fill 'er up, mister?"

"Huh? Yeah, sure, and top it off."

On the way home Brady fiddled with the radio, going from station to station, then switched it off and settled back, letting his thoughts take over.

It wasn't long until he arrived, but not ready to give up his thoughts, he drove up a hilltop road overlooking his home town and parked his car.

Brady's eyes sought the school building he had attended and the town's bustling main street, the old rodeo grounds and where other sports and special events took place. A quickening of breath made him groan aloud. These are good people, he thought. The salt of the earth. All they know is what we tell them. But what are we telling them? Is it all true?

These questions perturbed Brady, but as yet, he couldn't quite accept the duplicity Charity heaped upon Freeman. After all, any sane man wouldn't tell such lies; it would be murder. And Freeman was a general!

Brady let his eyes roam along the streets, finally resting on the road leading southeast out of town to his dad's place. He studied the house, saw the animals grazing, and a surge of peace filled his body. He loved the near isolation of this town, cupped by large hills on all four sides. For the first time Brady sensed a new vulnerability about his town that made him shiver. Could it really be, he wondered, that Charity is right? If she is right, he concluded, someone has to help.

Brady found himself anxious now to be with his own people, and reviving the motor, backed his car up and sped down the hill. As he came to a screeching halt in front of his house, the screen door opened, and his family came out decked in their Sunday attire. For a minute Brady could not believe his eyes! His father looked unnaturally taller because of the terrible gauntness that made his clothes hang ungainly over his bony frame. The twins still looked robust and unconcerned. Slowly, his mother walked towards him, stooping more noticeably than ever.

Jumping from the car, Brady was at their sides. After hugging his mother, he turned to his father. "Dad, are you all right?" Brady was shocked at the wrinkled man before him and at the dead look in the usually sharp eyes.

"I'm all right, Brady. Glad you could come." Jed's movements were slow and calculated now. It made Brady flinch, and he wanted to cry out.

"I'll drive you into St. George in my car," Brady spoke hurriedly.

"No!" Sarah's voice was quick and sharp, then she tried to smile. "Brady, dear, too much wind isn't good for your father."

"Then I'll drive Dad's car. You and Father get in back and the twins in front with me."

"Thank you, dear. It's nice to have you home again." Brady closed their door, walked around the car, and got behind the steering wheel.

"Brady," Jenny squealed, "you made the most beautiful cloud ever. It came right over our house this time!" Her excitement subsided some. "Mama wouldn't let any of us go outside though, and Papa had another dizzy spell."

Brady's thoughts skyrocketed back to yesterday's shot and the agitated concern Charity had shown.

"Brady," his sister exclaimed, "this one was a lot lower. Mama said the awful thing was never going to dis— dis—" The youngster looked beseechingly at her mother for help.

"Jenny, I said disperse."

"But it didn't, did it, Mama? Because it wasn't high enough to go over the hill." She settled back and snuggled close to her brother.

"Geepers, Brady," forced the usually subdued Jeremy, "Papa says he feels sure it's hurtin' everything. And poor Uncle Dale sure had been so sick." Young Jeremy courageously dashed at the threatening tears trickling past his nose, too much of a man to want to show his feelings.

Jed whispered, "It's true, Brady. Too many unusual things

are happening. Sheep bleeding from the nose, hundreds dying, deformed offspring, swathes of trees on our Taylor Grazing looking like a ravaging fire has hit them. You should see it yourself. Brady, if it was just hit and miss now and then, I'd think a bug or disease caused it. But not when it all comes at once and doesn't leave." Jed's voice was growing listless. "Four of our heifers died. No reason. Old Mert, the one we raised from a calf, bled to death before I knew what had happened. Four out of six newborn calves this year died. Bled to death. All I could do was watch them die." Jed's voice rang of defeat.

Brady drove up to the church and parked, then helped his parents out.

"Jed, I wish you'd not stay the two hours for the viewing. We could come back for the services." Sarah was worried.

"No, Sarah! Dale wasn't just my brother, but the best friend I ever had. I owe it to him and to myself to be here with him." Jed sounded gruff. "Dale wouldn't have left me, Mother."

"Very well, Jed. Just keep to my side."

"But, Dad. . . ," Brady interjected, "are you sure you feel all right? We could easily come ba. . . ."

"Brady," his father interjected, "no point in arguing. I'm staying!"

"Yes, sir!" Brady's reply was quick.

As the family moved into the mortuary, Brady looked around the room and started to shake hands with family and friends. It had been some years since he had seen most of them. He embraced his aunt and offered his condolences. He spoke sincerely about the beauty of flowers and also on the reverent strains of the organ. Then turning toward the bronze metal casket, he thought he would faint. This wasn't Uncle Dale! He felt like shouting aloud. My uncle was a robust, laughing man;

this is an old, shriveled-up skeleton of a man.

Brady looked quickly at his father and recognized the same changes taking place in him, too. My word! he thought. What is happening here? Carefully, he watched his father move to the casket. Jed leaned slightly toward the brother he had loved, and a calloused, work-weary hand brushed at his eyes as his lips trembled. He tried to stand straight but wobbled slightly. He turned abruptly and sought Sarah's eyes.

Aching to be alone, Brady walked out into the peaceful atmosphere of St. George and tried to bring some semblance of order to his chaotic feelings.

"Hi, Brady! Long time no see." A familiar voice startled him from behind.

"Dan! Dan Collins! Didn't see you inside." Brady shook his cousin's hand.

"Yes, it's been too long, I guess."

Brady looked his boyhood pal over. "Married I hear. An attorney, too, and no farming."

"That's right, Brady. No farm but a law degree. Just couldn't hack farming." They laughed together. "This is my oldest child, Tracy. She's five. I have two others, a boy nearly three and a baby, four months."

"Beautiful child, Dan."

"Yes, she is. She's always been Dad's pride and joy."

"Dan, how long had Uncle Dale been ill?" Brady's voice suddenly became serious. "He got very thin, didn't he?"

"Yah. About a year, I'd say. Maybe more. Thin you think? Yah, I guess he was." Dan's voice was reminiscent of the past. "Better get inside or Mother will be wondering where I am."

As Brady stood alone and watched his cousin walk inside, uneasiness and fear nearly tore him apart. Turning back inside, he stopped short, then moved quickly behind a tree. There, coming down the street was a car he could have spotted a mile away, its sleek black color gleaming in the sun's rays, the two one-foot stars and stripes fluttering in the breeze. A nasty tang came into his mouth.

Just for a second Brady's eyes looked into those of Dr. Phillips and recognition sparked. He saw Phillips was about to speak, but Brady turned abruptly. Again Charity's voice haunted him, "Doctor Phillips brought back reports that radiation in Alamo was a lot higher than anticipated." Doctor Phillips and General Freeman? Here, in St. George? Still Brady wasn't sure. I wonder if they have been to Alamo? Brady kicked at the grass, impatient now to get a few answers. But first he needed a good talk with his mother. His own family was far from well, and he wanted to know what was being done about it. And he wanted to know just what illness had destroyed his uncle. Charity's voice seemed to speak to him again, "Brady, I'm willing to bet your uncle died of cancer or leukemia." Resolved, he gritted his teeth and walked back into the mortuary.

CHAPTER 11

"Jedediah, dear. Go in and lie down until supper." Sarah hovered over her husband like a setting hen over her chicks. "Brady and the twins will do the chores."

"This time, woman, I'll do as you ask." He drew her to him. "I couldn't do without you, you know, don't you?"

"Yes," a sob escaped her lips.

Sarah gently pushed him toward the bedroom door, and as he left, she walked to the front porch where Brady and the twins were playing.

"Is he all right, Mom?" Brady drew his mother down onto the porch swing and put his arm around her.

"Heaven only knows. If only he would go to the doctor." Sarah stopped as she noticed the twins tuning in their ears to her. "Children, please run to the garden and pick the biggest corn you can find and bring some tomatoes and a cucumber or two."

Quick to obey they dashed off.

"Mom, just what was Uncle Dale's illness? Do you know what he died of?" Brady looked intently at his mother's stricken face as he asked the question that had been on his mind for days.

"Dale's insides were literally eaten away. It was a horrible death."

"Cancer?" Brady spoke low.

"Yes, Brady. But no one wanted to admit it."

He looked straight into his mother's eyes and spoke. "What do you mean, no one wanted to admit it?"

"Oh, Brady! I'm so afraid, and if you don't know by now. . . ." Sarah started to cry. "People are getting scared. We just don't know what to do!"

"But, Mom, just what do you mean, no one wanted to admit it? People all over the world die of cancer. Why is that hard to admit?"

Sarah looked hard at her son, her face lost its color, and her lips closed hard.

"I can't believe that you can be so naive about what's going on. Where are your eyes, Brady?" Sarah got up to go.

"Mom! Wait. . . ." Brady stood up, too. "Are you trying to say that the nuclear tests have something to do with these deaths, with cancer?"

"Yes. I'm saying the tests have something to do with it. Your Uncle Dale isn't the only one. There have been lots of others — friends I've had all my life. Cousins, children, even babies, and now," she choked as she fled back to the house, "it's your own father!"

Jed caught the hysterical woman as he came out the bedroom door. "Sarah! Get yourself together! Nothing's wrong with me but age and. . . ." He let his eyes drift to Brady, making him flinch. "At least Dale has one son to run his place now, even if Dan did run off to school and left him like you did me."

"Oh, Jed. How can you say such things?" Sarah exclaimed.

"Brady, your mother is hysterical over Dale's death. It will be worse now; everything will be blamed on the tests." His father tried a tired smile.

"Jed, you should be lying down."

"And now she wants to blame my problem on the tests." He lifted a trembling hand at Brady. "The problem here is a son who wouldn't help out when he was needed."

"Come on, Dad. Let's not get into this again. Not today of all days." Brady tried to soothe his father.

"No, son, I think this is a very good day for us to get at the bottom of our differences." Jed's ire started to get to him.

"Please. What's gotten into you anyway? You must go lie down." But Sarah's soothing words fell in deaf ears.

"Did either of you take a good look at Dale today?" Jed lashed out indignantly. "No, I don't suppose you would. But I did. Boy!" he said, pointing at Brady, "Dale was hardly in his fifties, and he looked a hundred and fifty!" Jed slumped a little upon Sarah. "You see what too much work does to you? Well, your cousin Dan ran out on Dale just like you did on me."

"Please, Dad. Let's not argue, you're ill. Why don't you go in the house and rest for a while." Brady went to his father and put his hand on his arm.

"I don't need your help or your sympathy. Just go back to your test site! We don't need you here!" He shook off Brady's hand.

"All right! I will!" Brady turned and started for the door when his mother's scream whirled him around.

"Brady! Your father!"

He rushed to her side, and together they carried Jed to the car and rushed him to the hospital. In the waiting room, Sarah tried to comfort her son, but consolation comes hard.

"It's all right, Brady. This would have happened anyway." Sarah looked fondly at her son. "Maybe his anger brought it on a little quicker, but I really think it was Dale's death.

They rose quickly as the doctor came into the room, and Sarah rushed at him.

"How is he, doctor?"

"Sarah, would you and Brady come into the consultation room for a few moments?" The doctor's voice was kind.

"Brady, bring up a chair for your mother." Looking directly at Sarah, he said, "Mrs. Collins, I know this comes as no surprise to you; we knew the day would come when this would happen."

"Come to this! What are you talking about?" Brady was on his feet instantly.

"Brady, your father has cancer." The doctor's voice was caring but matter-of-fact.

"Well, do something!" Brady shouted at the doctor.

"Brady, calm down! It's gone beyond help now. His condition is critical."

"Why is it critical? Apparently you've known for some time he's had cancer." Brady wouldn't accept the calmness of the doctor, and disbelief shown in his eyes. "There must be something you could have done."

"Yes, Brady, we have known for sometime he's had cancer, but. . . ." the doctor's groping for words forced Sarah to explain.

"Brady, dear, your father would do nothing about this. He refused to be treated."

"But why?" Brady turned on his mother.

"Your father is a very proud man and sometimes a stubborn one. He didn't want to be another person looked at as a victim of some atomic test." Sarah began to weep openly, then turned to the doctor. "I'm going to see Jed."

Again the doctor spoke to Brady, openly, "Your father is, indeed, a hard-headed, proud man. He wouldn't accept the fact that he was even ill; he couldn't bear the thought of possibly not being able to support his family. Brady, your mother got him to me once. If he'd cooperated, then he may have had a chance of living longer."

"Doctor, are you and Mom saying there is a chance that the atomic tests are to be blamed for Dad?"

"Brady, that is the question we would all like answered by the Energy Commission. All we get is, 'There's no danger.' But Brady, I'm sure there is. I've been practicing in St. George for a long time, and lately I've had to tell people who are my good friends that their fathers, mothers, sisters, brothers, and even their children and babies are facing tragic deaths. I can't be positive that those pinkish-orange clouds that pass over St. George are contaminating us. But I can say that never before have we had so many cancer deaths as we've had since those clouds have come."

The doctor shook his head. "There's something there, but I just don't know what."

Brady's face clouded with thoughts not to his liking, and he shook his head despondently. "I can't get all this, doctor, but I'm going to dig deeper and listen more. Do all you can for Dad and remember Mom and the twins, too."

"I know, Brady. And son. . . ." the doctor cleared his throat, "don't let your father's anger toward you upset you too much. He's a sick man. I'll watch out for your mother and the twins. Now, go see your father, Brady."

As they left Jed's room, Brady turned to his mother. His eyes were full of turmoil. "Mom, there's something I need to check out. I hate to leave like this, but I'll keep in touch. Okay?"

"Okay. I know you must," Sarah answered. Then her eyes

followed Brady, her heart aching, as he walked down the long corridor of the hospital.

CHAPTER 12

After leaving the hospital, Brady went straight home and walked into the empty house, going from room to room and ended up in the kitchen. Nothing seemed right, and a foreboding clamminess made him shiver. As was a long-standing habit, he picked up a glass and walked to the refrigerator. Taking a pitcher of milk out, he poured himself a drink. As the liquid started down his throat, Brady jumped to the sink and spit hard.

"Don't drink the milk!" Charity's face was undeniably before him, her voice alarmingly real.

"Sap!" He chastised himself. "Milk is the staff of life; everyone here drinks milk." Still, Brady couldn't bring himself to drink the milk his family was drinking daily.

Taking a glass jar from his mother's cupboard, he filled it with milk and secured the lid, then put the pitcher back into the fridge. Going to his room, he picked up his duffle bag and hurried from the house, the milk clutched tight.

The hundred and ninety-or-so miles from St. George to Mercury had never seemed so long before; Brady was eager to get to his lab. He was eager to see absolutely what the milk contained. Even though it was a little late as Brady drove up to the lab, he hurried into the building, picked up the phone, and dialed a number.

"Curtis," came the voice from the other end.

"Curtis. Brady here. Glad you are still in."

"Just leaving. Anything special?"

"Sure is. Can you come over here for a few minutes?" Brady's voice was urgent.

"Be right there."

Brady paced the floor, fearful of what he would find in the milk. As Curtis walked in, Brady had the milk in a beaker ready for the technician. "This is too important to be left until morning. Will you please run the usual tests for me, now?"

"Sure. I'll call you when I have the results." Curtis hurried away.

Brady sat at his microscope, busily running tests on soil and grasses he had also brought back from St. George. The ringing of the telephone made him jump. In his haste the receiver flew out of his hand.

"Nervous, Brady?" Curtis laughed into the phone. "Sounds like the joint is coming down."

"Naw. Just busy and clumsy." Brady held his tension in.

"You should be nervous, Collins. This milk is something else. Must have come from a cow at ground zero. Brady, you still there?"

"Yeah, I'm here. You guys ever run tests on grass or soil samples from towns around here?" Brady held his breath.

"Sure! We're doing that all the time." Then Curtis laughed, "What's all this about?"

"Uh, I've got to do a report. What have the results been?" Brady dreaded the answer.

"They vary, of course, from region to region and according to time factors. But generally the same results are as in this milk here — high levels of different radioactivity, usually strontium, are pretty normal."

"Where do your reports go, Curtis? To anyone in particular, or can anyone see them?" Brady tried to act unconcerned.

"The general. Oh, and Doctor Fuller has her nose in it, too. But Freeman is where it's funneled through for future reference and use."

"Thanks, Curtis. I owe you one. See ya around." Brady let out a groan as he sat down, trying to digest what he had just heard. He picked up the telephone, and as the night operator for the compound answered, he made his voice soft. "Mildred? This is Brady Collins. Have you seen Doctor Fuller around lately? — Lou's Diner! Thanks, Mildred."

As Brady entered the diner, he noticed Charity in a corner booth and hurried over to it.

"Brady, what's the matter with you? You look terrible." Glad but surprised to see him, Charity quieted as she saw the fear written on Brady's face.

"Worse than that, doctor — we've got to stop these tests!" In his anxiety Brady didn't see Freeman's Sergeant Mayfield sitting in the next booth.

"Brady, what's this all about?"

"Listen, Charity, you told me you had reasons to be suspicious. I want to hear those reasons and now!" Brady's voice was excited, and in his eagerness didn't notice Mayfield listening so intently.

"Brady, sit down please and let's get at this sensibly." She looked searchingly at him. "Do you understand completely what

77

you're getting into? This is serious business." She leaned close to him and whispered, "It's also very dangerous."

The sergeant tried to catch her last words but couldn't.

"Charity, my father is dying of cancer, and I think the bombs are responsible." His appeal was tragic. "Someone is going to pay for this."

"Please, Brady. You must be very careful. There is danger." Charity tried to calm him by grasping his hands, but Brady still was tensed up.

"I brought milk back from our cows and had it tested. You were right when you told Freeman that the radiation levels were higher than reported." He frowned. "The thing that troubles me most is that Freeman has known it all along!" Agony filled his eyes. "Charity, what are we dealing with?"

"Brady, there are other reports that Freeman has seen, reports that could shut down these tests for good if they went public." Charity felt compassion for her companion.

As a waitress came to their table, both fell silent. As the girl moved away again, they resumed talking, and Mayfield leaned forward, straining to listen.

"But the public doesn't get the correct information." Brady looked sick. "I could kick myself for letting that smooth-voiced, smiling hyena dupe me like he has."

"Don't be too hard on yourself, Brady. He has the same effect on everyone." She tried to assure him.

"But you've known his true colors all along," he moaned.

"For quite sometime, Brady, and I've known that the true reports are being stopped."

"By General Freeman, Charity?" he interrupted her. "I'd like to see these reports if you have them."

"I have them. I get a set, just as Freeman does." She sighed.

"It will be a great relief for someone else to know all this."
Charity got up, ready to leave. "Come, they're at my office."

Brady paid for her bill, and they hurried to the car.
Mayfield followed at a discreet distance, careful not to be seen.

Charity took a key from her purse and opened her office
door. Going to the file cabinet, she took out another key and
opened it, pulling out a drawer.

"I've been afraid lately that my office would be broken into.
These reports are from some of the top men in their fields — Dr.
Finn, Dr. Wilcox, Dr. Mathews, and Dr. Sheldon."

"I recognize the names, but they don't work on the atomic
project anymore." Brady looked confused.

"No, Brady, they don't," Charity answered. "These reports
would have put a damper on the project because of the evidence
they presented against the atmospheric tests." Charity was
excited.

"And so they were dismissed." Brady's face was a study of
thought. "I guess that's why they brought in Doctor Phillips."

"Yes." Charity hesitated. "But I don't think Hugh is in on it.
I think he is an honest man — he hasn't run up against Freeman
too much." Taking the file out, she handed it to Brady. "Look
them over carefully, Brady, and I'm sure what you read will
make you sick." Intent on what they were doing, the two paid no
attention to the sound of silent footsteps that stopped just outside
the door.

"Brady, all these reports are authentic, and now I'm glad
you, too, will have the evidence. These last two years have been
tough. I've tried hard to get someone to wake up and face the
facts. Freeman has fought me all the way." Charity looked up,
and her body stiffened. Poking at Brady, she pointed to the
door and the shadow of a man silhouetted in the glass of the

door.

Brady got to his feet carefully and made his way to the door. Throwing it wide open, Brady caught a glimpse of a running figure as it darted around a corner. Charity stood shaking visibly, the color fading from her face.

"Brady, I — I don't like any of this. There's a conspiracy going on."

"Conspiracy! Do you know what you're saying?" Brady shook her gently.

"Yes, I think Freeman is only a part of it. Brady, I have never really been frightened before, but now," she shivered. "I haven't told anyone, but my movements have been monitored. My office has been meticulously searched, but so far they haven't tried to force my file cabinet."

"Are you sure?"

"Sure I'm sure!" Charity shot back at him. "That isn't all either. I've been followed, and even my apartment has been broken into." Charity looked hard at Brady, then smiled a crooked smile. "And haven't you heard the latest? 'Doctor Charity Fuller is completely schizoid.' "

"Charity! How ridiculous!" Brady laughed.

"Ridiculous?" She blew a winsome smile at him. "Doctor Fuller is ready for the nut house and the high walls," Charity mockingly related. "Anyway, I'll be removed before long, and another will take my place." She grew more serious. "I've failed as far as St. George, Alamo, and the other towns close to them are concerned." She locked the files away again and tapped the file cabinet.

"Doctor Fuller, I think what you need most is a short vacation. What would you think of a rendezvous in the desert?" Brady watched her face closely, "and with one Brady Collins, research scientist?"

Charity looked at Collins and felt the shackles that bound her slowly fall away. Disbelief, hope, then slowly a smile of happiness radiated from her countenance.

"Brady, you are one in a million."

"One in your lifetime is good enough for me." Brady's grin widened.

"When?" Charity's voice was low.

"How about tonight? You won't be held up, and it's still early." Her laugh was spontaneous and spread to Brady.

CHAPTER 13

As usual the guard was there to check Brady in, and as he came to a halt before Charity's apartment, he hurriedly got out of his car. As Brady raised his hand to knock, he was still mentally going over the things he'd bought for the trip when the door flung wide, and his knock was on air.

"Ready?" His question was needless as Charity stood elegantly before him in boots and jeans. He grinned, then said calmly, "Charity, better bring along a change and overnight bag."

"You're kidding!" Her face registered disbelief.

"Trust me, Miss Fuller."

Charity left him standing as she vanished behind the bedroom door and was back as quickly as she had gone.

"Ready, Brady, and I don't guess you'd tell me where to if I asked?"

"Nope! Secret's all mine." Brady helped her into the car, and they turned toward Vegas. Taking I-15, they raced along, the wind whipping at them. Charity raised her hands to her hair and letting it down, shook her head vigorously. Turning sparkling eyes to her companion, her voice came huskily, "This is heaven, Brady. I've been tied up way too long."

Brady's heart raced as he looked at her, and they drove on in silence.

"Valley of Fire?" Charity's voice was part question, part eagerness as she read the sign at the turn-off.

"Ever been there?" Brady cocked his head, looking at her.

"No-o-o, but I've heard others talk." Charity smiled.

"Well, I hope it's the diversion you need." Brady grew serious. "I used to play here as a little boy. It's beautiful."

As the car slowed down, Charity became erect.

"Brady, I can't believe all this fiery red!" Disbelief brought an ah to her lips.

"Charity, where are you from, anyway?" Brady asked.

"I'm from upstate New York, and I've never imagined, let alone seen, anything like this. This is all rock, isn't it?"

"Look over here. See all those sharp points. We used to call those the devil and his imps." Brady was in seventh heaven.

"Can we stop?" Charity was at the edge of her seat.

"Would you like to explore, Charity?" Brady teased.

"I would! Brady, please!"

His head went back, and he chuckled. "So, the lady says please. Well, let's see what's around."

The car shot off on a side road and came to stop at a rest area. Getting out, he helped Charity out. Waving his hand, he gestured, "Well, what would you like to do first?"

"Let's go hiking, Brady. I never have climbed rocks like these."

"Okay with me," Brady said with a laugh. "Mind my telling tales?"

"Do, please!"

"Well, St. George, where I come from, is surrounded by

hills like these, too. One day two of my buddies dared me to climb one of the steepest ravines. Like a sap, I couldn't say no. Well, the time came when it was easier to go on than turn back. About halfway up, as I regained my footing after stepping over a rock, there, no more than three feet away, was an eighteen-inch Gila monster, his eyes locked into mine. Whew! I'd run into those babies before, and I knew they were deadly poison. I also knew they were slow and awkward." He glanced at Charity, and the horror upon her face made him laugh. Taking her by the shoulders, his voice was light. "Come on! I'm alive, aren't I?"

Charity rested her head against his chest, her hair falling about her face, reaching nearly to her waist. He felt her body quiver and drew her close.

"Are there many of those things around here?" her voice shook.

"Some — and turtles — but nothing to worry about." His voice gave her assurance. "Want to still explore?"

"Yes, I would. Maybe it will get the knots out of my insides."

For an hour they climbed, skidded down rocks, tramped over sand. New color flushed into her face. Finally they reached the top of a hill, and as Charity's gaze wandered over the hills, she threw her arms wide, "Brady, isn't this glorious! What colors!"

"Yah, we have every color imaginable." He spoke with some pride.

The moon had risen high before Brady got the warm fire cracking to scare out the chill of the desert night. Nudging closer to the fire, Charity sat up, knees under her chin, and lost herself in dreams.

Brady spread out full-length on his side and watched the fire reflect in her eyes.

"Brady, I want to apologize for the way I've treated you in the past." Her eyes sought his.

"Ah, forget it," Brady grinned.

"No, I mean it; I've been a real pain for you. I've been cold, suspicious, even uncooperative — I'd say downright obnoxious. I hated you for a time when I thought you were a stooge for Freeman."

"That was a long time ago, Charity. Now let's start over."

They looked at each other, and the fire brought an added glow to their faces.

"Well, Charity," he drawled, "it's nice to really meet you — at last." Getting to his feet, he offered his hand and pulled her to her feet.

"Thank you for taking me here tonight, Brady."

"Well, we've still got tomorrow and Sunday — we're going places and doing things. Is it a deal?"

"It's a deal!" They shook hands.

"Now, how about dessert?" Brady's grin was mischievous.

"Dessert?" Charity repeated. "Where would it come from?"

"Oh, it's one of the desert's gifts to man," he taunted.

"Are you serious?" Her eyes tried to read his meaning.

"Of course, I'm serious. Nothing better than rattlesnake meat or lizard. . . ."

"Bur-r-r!" Charity was in his arms before he knew it. The impact caught him off guard, and he drew her close to him. They laughed, then silence came between them, deep and penetrating. Their eyes locked. Brady's hand went to her hair and pushed a lock from her face. Her eyes were large and questioning.

It was Brady who broke the silence. "I think it's time we were on our way."

Charity lowered her head and a soft "Thank you" was barely audible. She followed him to the car, and soon they were again on their way.

Perhaps an hour and a half went by before Charity recognized the area.

"Brady, are we going to St. George?"

"Yep, my mom is one in a million; you'll like her."

"But, Brady, unannounced, and at night? She'll think it scandalous."

"Charity, just you be quiet." Brady's hand went out to hers, and with a squeeze he chuckled, "This will take her mind off my dad. I've told you she's taking it hard."

Hardly had the car come to a halt when the screen door to the front porch banged and squeals rent the air.

"Brady! Brady! Mama, it's Brady!" The young twins came flying to the car, but their mouth's clamped shut and their eyes grew large as they noticed he wasn't alone.

Jenny, fingers in her mouth, went to her brother, while Jeremy went bursting into the house shouting, "Mom, Brady has a lady with him."

Sarah Collins, busy with lap mending, put her work aside, and brushing at her hair and straightening her apron, she put out her hand to her younger son and smiled. "Perhaps it's Doctor Charity. I hope so; he has mentioned her a lot."

Going to the car, Sarah smiled at the shyness of the woman at her son's side.

"Brady, dear, you couldn't have come at a better time and how wonderful that you would bring such a lovely guest." Sarah's voice was soothing and her eyes appealing. "Do come in. I'll fix you both something to eat."

"I'm delighted to meet you, Mrs. Collins, even if it is so late.

I told Brady it was asking too. . . ."

"Oh," came Sarah's voice, "on the farm, hours don't count. You won't mind if I call you Charity, I hope." Sarah's eyes sparkled. "You see, my son talks about you so much I feel as if I know you."

Charity was benumbed by Sarah's graciousness and could only smile her consent.

Carefully, Brady asked, "How's Dad doing?"

"No better — he never complains." Sarah led them into the front room where Jedediah Collins sat in a recliner. Seeing Brady, he struggled to get up.

"How are you, Dad?" Brady shook his father's hand. "Dad, I'd like you to meet one of my bosses." Turning to Charity, he grinned. "Charity Fuller, my father."

Charity scrutinized the man before her, her emotions building as the past worries of the atomic tests mounted again inside her.

"Brady talks of you constantly, Mr. Collins. I'm very pleased to meet you."

"Brady, it's about time you brought a young woman home." Jed's voice sounded happily animated for the first time in months. "Thought the young pup would never wake up."

Charity blushed, and Brady stood slightly embarrassed, a twinkle in his eyes. Sarah put a restraining hand out to her husband. "Jed, dear, you'll frighten Charity away."

"Nonsense, woman — any lass likes a little lemon in her cup of tea." Turning toward Charity, he smiled. "Isn't that right?"

"Absolutely!" Charity grinned her acceptance of Brady's family.

As Charity looked about the immaculate, well-organized house, she sensed it was a home in every way; vibrations of love, warm and secure, filled its interior. She knew this family was special. And Brady? Charity looked at him, and her heart missed a beat.

"Brady, dear, take the lovely doctor up to the north bedroom. The cross breeze there is refreshing." Sarah smiled at Charity. "I must see that Father gets to bed."

Jeremy started out with Charity's overnight case, but Brady stopped him. "Whoa there, young fella. This is my job — someday perhaps." Brady grinned, and Jeremy squirmed.

As Brady showed Charity about the small home, they ended up at the guest bedroom, and opening the door, he turned on the light.

"Clean as a room before army inspection." Brady laughed as they looked at each other. Slowly drawing her to him, he whispered, "Sleep well, Charity, and good night."

"Thank you for everything," Charity whispered back, kissing him on the cheek. "I will."

CHAPTER 14

Brady donned his old clothes and slipped quietly from the house in the early morning. After ten years' absence from the farm, he wondered if his hands could still milk cows. In a way Brady missed the farm life and all its back-breaking labor. It was in him, he couldn't deny it, but still he knew it wasn't what he wanted in life. Hardly had Brady finished feeding the animals when he was startled by his father's voice.

"What you doing up so early, son? Thought you came to relax."

"Naw, I came to let Dr. Fuller unwind." Brady tried to see the expression in his father's eyes. "The test site and all the bombs going off were getting to her."

"She's pretty, son, but needs more meat. I hope she likes us as a family." Jed's voice was careless and gentle.

"She's from New York state, Dad, and never been on a farm. I don't know how she'll like it."

Brady was a little surprised to find himself wondering and hoping so much that Charity would enjoy her stay with the family. But deep down he was pretty sure she would.

"Why so silent, boy. The world's come awake." Jed's chiding

jolted Brady, making his heart jump.

"Thinking, Dad. Just thinking." Brady wasn't sure just how long he'd been silent.

"Well, don't think too long, boy. The ship might pass you by." They looked at each other tenderly, and a flash of understanding flitted across each face.

"Glad you came, son. I — I've. . . ." Jed's voice faltered.

"Me, too, Dad," Brady broke in, not wishing his father to become too emotional.

"I've missed all this — I really like coming home."

"I'm glad to hear that. Your mother is going to need more than the little tykes, you know."

"I know," was all Brady said, not wanting to bring up again the subject of why he left.

The sun was just over the hill as the two men entered the kitchen, milk pails in hand. Brady watched Charity as she helped his mother.

"Well, close your mouth, Brady Collins. I am a woman, you know." Her teasing was spontaneous and light. "I heard you sneak out, and I also heard your mother rustling in the kitchen. I just couldn't stay in bed. Now come and eat."

It seemed too soon to Charity when Brady announced they must leave. To her, this family had struck beneath the surface. Never had she felt so completely in tune with life. The family's naturalness and deep love for each other captivated her completely.

Saying goodbye was a peculiar experience to Charity. She wanted to stay — she wanted to laugh — she wanted to cry. Never had this happened to her before. As an only child of professional people, life had been a challenge, something to conquer, or die; no deep-rooted love between people like she

found here. Charity looked about the kitchen and studied Sarah
Collins, embodiment of all the word mother stood for: gentle,
kind, considerate, and forgiving. Never had she known a woman
so brave and genteel. Going to Sarah, Charity put out her hand
and started to thank the older woman, but Sarah embraced her
instead.

"Charity, it's been wonderful having you. Thank you for
coming." Sarah then embraced Brady and tried to cover her
tears. "Be away with you, dear."

As the car sped down the highway, Charity broke into
silence.

"Brady, your mother is a very brave woman. I couldn't help
but love her dearly. The agony she lives each day, knowing in a
matter of weeks, even days, her husband will no longer be with
her. . . ," Charity looked away from Brady, and her voice
dropped low. "How she must suffer, seeing him slowly fade
away." After a few minutes, she turned to him again and
hesitantly asked, "Did you say anything to them about the milk?"

"No!" The crack of his voice was like a pistol shot. "How
could I say anything? It's their livelihood. They drink it all the
time. All of St. George drinks their milk." His hands clenched
upon the steering wheel. "Charity, it's pure agony knowing what
we know and being so helpless. I'm just waiting for the next
session with Freeman."

"Do you believe for one minute Freeman will change the
course he is bent on following?" Charity asked caustically.

Brady looked deep into her eyes, the agony of
determination blanching his face.

"There must be something we can do. And whatever it is,
we'll have to act fast."

Charity only stared blankly down the desert road wondering

to herself if they *could* stop Freeman.

A couple of hours later they stopped before Charity's apartment, and Brady walked her to the door.

"It's been a wonderful two days, Brady. I wish there could be more."

"There will be, I promise." He drew her close and kissed her softly on the lips. Then he moaned, "I'd better go, but I'll see you in the morning. The meeting, you know."

"Oh, that's right. We do have a meeting, don't we? It's the Scorpio shot, isn't it?" She frowned hard. "Wish the general would go up with it."

"Now, don't get angry. We have to stay cool. We're in this together, okay?" Brady noticed her shiver.

"Okay. It does lessen the tension knowing that you're with me."

"See you in the morning." He kissed her again lightly, then turned and walked away.

Charity stood in the doorway and watched Brady walk off. For the first time in her life she found herself caring and worrying about a man and wishing he didn't have to leave her.

CHAPTER 15

Hardly had Brady fallen asleep when the alarm brought him up pawing the air. Arriving at the conference room, Brady found Charity was already there, and as he shot her a quick glance, he felt rejuvenated by her pert and cool look.

"Good morning, Mr. Collins," her voice was cool. "Glad to see you here."

"Doctor." Brady's face was straight as he acknowledged her greeting. "It was a short night, but I'm here as you can see."

"I'm delighted." She put her hand out to him. "Shall we join the others? It looks as if Freeman is chafing at the bit — don't want to rile him so early in the morning."

They chose seats at the table facing each other. Brady looked around. The usual people were there, along with Freeman's aides. His eyes turned to Charity, and a wink made a slow blush steal over her face. As she lowered her head, Brady smiled to himself.

"If it isn't asking too much for small talk to cease, I'd like to bring this meeting to order," General Freeman's voice suddenly boomed. "As you know, Scorpio has been scheduled. It appears that wind conditions will be in our favor at the time of the blast."

As he spoke, fire rushed in his veins, making his voice nearly hypnotic. "Your dedication to this work really makes you true Americans," his beady eyes roamed the room. "If I may have your attention, I have other things to say; things quite pertinent to what's going on here at the test site." His irritation brought bright color to his face.

"General," Brady's voice full of vim brought an instant hush to the room. "I have a question to ask before we start."

Eyes piercing, the general let Brady's request be aired. "What is so important, Collins, that you request time now?"

"General, I had tests run on some milk samples that I brought from St. George. The particles count was found to be higher than what we've been led to believe the radiation levels actually are."

"And just where are your reports, Mr. Collins?" A sneer twitched at the general's mustache.

Brady glared at the general and ignored the interference. "General, that means that the radiation is not dispersed as well as we had thought and that it is contaminating for longer periods of time than we supposed." Brady looked about the room, letting his words register upon the minds of those present. He looked at Charity last, and the sparkle in her eyes brought him new confidence. "General, if the milk is affected, then the cows are picking up particles from the grass and passing them on through the environmental chain to people."

"Collins," the general nearly roared, and his fist came down hard upon the table, "before you sling accusation around here, you'd better have proof."

"I have my proof, General, and now I'd like my answers." Brady grew almost belligerent.

"I'm warning you, Collins. I'm in command here —

produce your proof," the general smirked.

"It's filed with the lab. Curtis ran it for me. He has it."
Brady looked around the table again, this time his eyes lingered
upon Charity; a new look of fear had enveloped her face, and
her sparkle had vanished.

One of Freeman's aides left the room and returned in
twenty minutes from what should have been a five minute walk.
Curtis was with him, his head slightly bowed. Brady looked at
Charity, a question in his eyes, and she shrugged her shoulders.

"Mr. Curtis," Freeman's tone was cocky, "I'm told Mr.
Collins gave you milk samples to run for radioactivity. Do you
have the information?"

"No, sir."

"You liar!" Brady jumped to his feet. "You ran those tests!
You told me it must have come from ground zero it was so badly
contaminated — you. . . ."

"Thank you, Mr. Curtis." Freeman's cool exterior was
infuriating. Turning his polished smile upon those assembled, he
continued, "Gentlemen, I have no explanation for what you've
heard here. And as for you, Mr. Collins, I cannot understand
just what you are trying to do." He looked at Brady with a
bemused smile. "I'll just have to blame it on stress." He gave a
thin smile at Charity and chuckled.

"Freeman, how many have you railroaded out of here
besides Doctors Sheldon, Finn. . . ." the general cut him short.

"That's all, Collins. I could get you for insubordination."
Looking at Dr. Fuller, he sneered. "I'm sorry, gentlemen. We'll
recess for, say, half an hour, then come back, and we'll get down
to work."

Freeman stood at attention until the room emptied, then he
froze Brady and Charity with his pale blue eyes before leaving.

"No one is going to deter me from my cause."

Brady reached across the table and took Charity's hand and gave it a reassuring squeeze. "It's all right, Charity. We aren't down yet, and for sure there's something going on here that just isn't right." Trying to make her smile, he flipped at her nose. "It's more than Freeman. He has at least two stooges, Mayfield and Curtis."

"Brady," Charity whispered cautiously, "I'm afraid for you now, too. Freeman is deadly. He knows we know too much — even to have us fired."

"Chin up, fair lady; he isn't that desperate, I hope."

"Brady, I've seen him act before." Charity got to her feet and walked to the window. "I'm handing in my resignation."

"You can't do that — not until we stop Freeman and these open shots — something has to be done. We must think of all those towns out there." His voice was desperate. "My dad is dying, my uncle is dead. Who's next, Charity?"

"I can't stay here, Brady. I will not face Freeman or another one of his sham reports." Turning to him, she gave him a tired smile. "I'm leaving, Brady. Are you coming with me?"

"No, Doctor Fuller, I'm not." His voice was hard. "I'll face Freeman down." Putting his hands in his pockets, he paced the floor in deep thought. "Charity, I *must* stay. It's the Scorpio shot the general is talking about. We must know just what he intends to do."

"You're right, Brady. I'd forgotten about the Scorpio test. I'd *have* to stay if you didn't." As she walked away, an air of dejection followed her.

Brady stood rooted to the spot; never before had he wanted to rush to a woman and enfold her, giving her encouragement and comfort. With a stunned look on his face, he turned and looked out the window to the vast desert below.

Two hours later Brady let himself into his apartment, and after locking his door picked up the phone and dialed. "Yes, Mildred, please, for me honey, ring Dr. Fuller." He wheedled, "I realize it's late, but it's about the test shot coming up. Thank you, I'll hold."

A sleepy voice came to him, "Fuller speaking — Brady!" Her voice was electrified. "What is it?"

"Calm down, it's about Scorpio. It's scheduled for Wednesday, 0600." His voice was like music to her ears. "Sorry to butt in on your sleep."

"Brady, it was worth it. I couldn't sleep anyway," she broke into his talk.

"Well, maybe now you'll sleep better. Remember Wednesday."

Brady's head had hardly hit the pillow it seemed when his room suddenly went alight, and a stupendous explosion brought him leaping to the window. Pulling the curtains wide, he looked into the brilliantly lighted sky and shivered. The orange-red illuminated everything for miles around.

"This can't be!" Brady croaked as he stumbled to the phone. "Mildred, this is Collins. Ring Dr. Fuller for me — and hurry!" As the phone clicked, he exclaimed, "Charity, this is Brady. Did you see it?"

"Yes, Brady, but I'm not surprised," her voice had a hollow ring.

"Not surprised? What do you mean? Scorpio wasn't due 'till Wednesday," Brady shouted.

"Calm down. This isn't the first time unscheduled shots have been conducted. Freeman does as he wishes."

"Charity, I'm going to St. George. If I can't stop Freeman here, maybe I can get people there to wake up to what's going on. See you in a couple of days. And, Charity, do be careful."

In minutes Brady roared down the road until ahead of him a long line of stopped cars appeared. Seeing no reason for the delay, Brady weaved in and out of traffic before eyeing a check point ahead. Backing up, he crossed over to the wrong lane and began dodging the oncoming cars. A man at the check point saw Brady coming up the wrong side of the road and yelled to his assistant, "Hey, Banner! Looks like we've got a problem coming our way! Get him and fast!"

"Crazy dope. Always some loony to spoil the night. He's either drunk or crazy. Hey, you! Stop!"

Brady stopped short, glaring at the officer.

"You in a hurry, buddy," leered the guard.

"Sure am! My wife is having our overdue Siamese twins, and I got to get to her." Brady thumped the steering wheel hard.

"Well, we can't let you pass until your car is washed off."

"What's this all about?" Brady frowned.

"Safety measures. Nuclear test west of here tonight and we always have to wash the dust from the cars, you understand?"

"No, I don't understand," Brady flashed back. "I work at the test site, and they say there isn't any fallout this far out."

"I don't care if you are the President of the United States, I got orders, and I'll enforce them even if. . . ."

"Orders!" Brady shouted as a crowd gathered about, listening. "*Orders* from whom?"

"Since you work at the test site, I guess you'd recognize the name of the top brass. How about General George Freeman himself?"

"Do I know Freeman!" Brady roared. Brady looked about

and noticed a small stream. "Is that where the water drains from all this washing?"

"Yah. Sure is handy, don't you think?" Cockiness shone upon Banner's face.

"And where does this stream go?" Brady's voice was like chipped ice.

"Why, down the valley, can't you see?"

"Yes, indeed! I do see! And I also see this water as the main stream to the crops, cattle, and in some instances drinking water of the innocent people below." Brady was red hot by now. "You and Freeman are deliberately feeding what he calls harmless fallout to people. Yet it's deadly enough on a crummy car that it can't go into another state without being washed off."

"I — I. . . ," Banner stuttered. "I didn't think — Freeman is such a big shot, and we obey orders." The crowd had enlarged and was buzzing.

"This boy giving you trouble, Banner?" The other guard came up, not liking what he had seen.

"Not exactly," Banner frowned. "He just told me something I don't like about washing these cars and letting the water drain into this stream."

"Let him pass," the command came clipped from the other officer. "We have troubles enough."

CHAPTER 16

Brady came to a screeching halt in the driveway in front of the farm house and saw his mother coming to him.

"Brady, dear," tears flowed freely, and her fragile body shook with emotion. "We had to put your father in the hospital again. It won't be long for him now."

"When did you take him to the hospital?" Brady stood dazed.

"Last night — doctor says he's not sure how much time there is."

"Could I go see him now?" Brady looked stricken.

"Yes, doctor said anytime, day or night." Sarah struggled for control. "Your father wouldn't let me call you. Brady, he loves you deeply, but he is such a proud man. Go to him."

Brady knew his mother felt it would be his last chance for him to really talk to his father.

As Brady walked down the corridor of the hospital, it was with trepidation that he paused at the door of his father's room. Glad that it was closed, he breathed deeply, then gently pushed it open. Seeing the slim figure in the bed, he wanted to cry out in protest. Noting the sunken eyes were closed, he started to shut the door in retreat, thinking his father asleep.

"Brady, please come in." Just audible was his father's voice.

"Dad!" Brady almost choked. "How are you?"

"Not too good, son. I don't know how long I have." He looked at his boy. Lifting a trembling arm, he motioned Brady closer. "Come in, boy. I want to look at you good."

"Don't talk like that, Dad. I know what you're made of. You're a lot tougher than that."

"Brady, I want to make things right with you."

"Dad, things *are* right!"

"No, they're not, boy. I have been very harsh with you, especially these past few years." He searched his son's face. "I've been sharp with your mother, too. It's these things I regret now. Too late to amend for the sorrow I've caused — but not to admit it — and ask for forgiveness."

Brady couldn't take all this from his father — the man who used to be so iron-willed. He leaned over the bed, letting his head fall on his father's chest, and cried as he had done many times as a boy.

"Brady, I wouldn't let myself believe what I knew about this fallout until Dale succumbed to it. I just couldn't believe it." His breath was laborious. "Even when the doctor told me, I was still stubborn."

"Dad! Dad!" was all Brady could say.

"Boy, it was much easier to blame you and your mother than to blame strangers in Washington and what they were doing to us at the test site. Can you forgive me?"

"Oh, Dad, and all this time I thought. . . ," Brady raised his head unashamed as tears glistened in his eyes.

"Boy, I want you to know deep down inside I've been real

proud of you and your accomplishments. I think in my bragging I've busted a few buttons off my shirts." Jed held tight to his son's hand.

"Thank you, Dad. All this time I've wasted thinking you didn't care," a peace came into Brady's heart.

"Thank you, Brady, for being my son." Breath was coming hard now. "Love your mother, son. She needs you. Be gentle to her — love her for me."

"Dad, oh, Dad, you have always been there. You mustn't give up now; we all need you."

The nurse poked her head around the door, and seeing Brady, walked to the bed. "It's time for your medication, Mr. Collins. You must get some rest and sleep."

"See you tomorrow, Dad. I'm here for a few days."

"I'm glad; laying here won't be so hard now, knowing you're with the family."

Brady stroked his father's brow, then leaned over and gave him a kiss. "Tomorrow, then, Dad."

Brady almost collided with a man as he hurried down the hall, tears dimming his vision.

"Hold on there, Brady Collins. It's been ages since I last saw you." The man touched his arm.

Brady looked at him with blank eyes.

"I see you've forgotten me, Brady." A laugh came from thin lips. "I don't blame you. I'm Trevor Johnson; we went to high school together."

"Trevor Johnson!" A wail tore from Brady's lips. "It can't be! What happened to you?" Brady knew Trevor was a year younger than he, but this man was old — his face pocked and skin discolored. He was ghastly looking, and his bones protruded from under loose skin. He supported himself with crutches.

"Come to my room, Brady. I've got a story to tell you — one that isn't pretty." Trevor hobbled in front of Brady. It took Trevor a few minutes of awkward struggle to settle himself on the bed. "It's been a long time, Brady," Trevor sighed.

"Yah, it has at that." Brady studied his friend for a few minutes. "What did you do when you finished school?" Brady was interested.

"I went into the army," Trevor almost hissed.

"What's wrong with that?" Brady came back at him. "I did, too. Only I went in at seventeen. My dad signed for me."

"Yah, I remember now — you went in for chemistry or science; you were always a whiz at that." Trevor grew serious. "But take me, just an ordinary soldier taking what the brass dished out. And look at me now."

"You mean the military did this to you?" Brady's mind whirled.

"Yah, I thought I was going to come out in a few years and have it made," Trevor cursed. "Now I'm dying. And when I'm gone — well. As far as the military goes, I'm not even on their records."

"You're kidding?" Brady sat stupified.

"Everything was fine until our unit got orders to go into the desert for some kind of nuclear training exercises. My company was chosen to man the trenches around the spot where they were going to drop an atom bomb. After the explosion, we were supposed to walk across ground zero."

Brady sat close to the edge of his chair, his hair standing on end as chills raced up and down his spine.

"I was nervous, standing there knowing we were all in danger, and I yelled out at the sergeant, 'I wish they'd get this thing over with,' I said."

103

" 'Shut up, Johnson,' he told me, 'The show will start soon enough.' Then he barked again, 'We go in thirty seconds. Get ready.' "

"Some of the soldiers jumped out of our trench and ran to trenches on the sides as the sergeant gave the command to move out. We spread out and turned our backs to ground zero."

"'Now remember,' I can almost hear his voice now, 'no matter what, don't look into the blast,' the sergeant commanded us. Then wham! The trenches seemed to be nothing but white heat, and the explosion and roar were worse than an earthquake. 'Help' I yelled loud. The roar increased, and it seemed like everything broke loose. Rocks, dirt, everything was coming at once." Fear contorted Trevor's face. "I couldn't stand the agony any longer so I raised myself to look out. Too late. I saw the earth rippling like waves on the sea and BAM! I went down like I was shot. Next thing I knew the sergeant was bending over me. I was bleeding like a stuck pig and half crazed I fought him off. 'Hank! Heywood! Miller! Help me get this dog, or he'll get us all!' I shouted." Trevor was half out of bed when his voice stopped, and he gazed at Brady. Wiping his face, he fell back, utterly spent. "It was horrible, Brady. And just when we thought the horror was over, the noise started all over again, and the quaking and roaring came at us again. This time the sarg looked over the trench, and that time he went flying against the dirt. I saw he was unconscious. All I thought about was to get help."

Brady put a hand on his friend. "Please, Trevor. You're shaking. Forget it."

"*Forget,* Collins! I stumbled into another trench and what a sight! No movement and the smell of burning flesh. Never again do I want to witness such horror! We didn't know the returning shock wave was deadly, too."

"What about the men, Trevor? Can you remember?" Brady felt sick.

"Sure. A lot got hurt pretty bad, and I don't know how many got killed. The military brass says none, but, Collins, I know that's a lie! I know what I saw, and I ain't crazy." Trevor sat up. "Brady, problem is, you can't find the records of any of us in the outfit. Like mine, they say all the records got burned in a fire at the base." Trevor looked at Brady.

"They have no records of your service?" Brady showed his astonishment.

"That's right. Completely vanished. As far as the army is concerned, I never was there." A sneer twisted his lips. "Enough of me, Brady. What about you? What are you doing?"

"I don't know, Trevor. I really don't know." As Brady looked at the old man before him, he shivered. "See you later, Trevor. I need to talk to a man."

As Brady drove into the yard again, he lingered outside, trying to get his thoughts together as he headed home.

"Brady," his mother's voice called him from the front door.

"Yes, Mom, I'm coming." He put his arm about her shoulders, and they walked into the house. "Mom, I need to call Grant Sayers; it's important."

"Sure, dear. You know where the phone is." As Sarah worked quietly about the kitchen, her ears were listening to her son's conversation.

"Sure, Grant. I tell you it's all true. Yes, I've told you the complete story. Now can you get it printed? No, it's not just hearsay. Listen, I can get you copies of the reports done by the researchers I've named. They all agree that the standards of radiation exposure are far too low and that people are getting lethal doses around here. Sure I can get you copies. Yes, I've read them myself. Fine. I'll get you the reports, and you print the story. Thanks, Grant." Brady dropped his head into his hands and only wished he had called sooner.

CHAPTER 17

Brady had another sleepless night but was up before dawn doing what he could about the farm before going back to the house for a hot breakfast.

"Brady, it isn't necessary for you to stay here. I'm not helpless." Sarah reached a hand out to him. Brady took her hand and squeezed it hard.

"Mom, you're the greatest — but I came to spend a few days with you. There are a few things I want to do yet."

"I guess we must learn to do — do without your father." Tears glistened in Sarah's eyes, and a quiver touched her lips. "I'd give anything if — if it would bring your dear, sweet father back." Emotions tore at her.

"Mom, what has happened cannot be recalled, but I'm going to do my best to see that it doesn't continue." He looked grim. "After seeing my friend Trevor Johnson, plus the rest, I want to get Freeman for good."

"Brady, dear, please be careful. I don't want you hurt."

"Why, Mom! It would take ten generals like Freeman to hurt me," Brady flared.

"But if this general is what you say he is, cowards don't work alone." She showed fear.

"Nah, there's too much at stake for the general. He loves his medals too much," Brady shrugged. "Come on, let's forget that for today. Right now I want to just please you!" He kissed her gently as he drew her to her feet.

"Thanks, dear. I'll just brush up a bit, can't have a dirty house. Then I'll freshen up myself, and we'll go to town."

It was well into the afternoon when Brady, again, brought his car to a stop before the farm house.

"Thank you, Brady, for all you've done for me today. You've spent a lot of money."

"No sweat, Mom; my bank balance is still in the seven digit line," he teased.

"Thank you again anyway."

"Mom, if you wouldn't feel too badly, I'd like to get back to the test site. I'd like to call Doctor Fuller first. I need information she has."

"Brady, dear, she is such a nice girl. Do bring her home again, and you know I'll be fine." Her thoughts were scattered. "Dear, she is right for you."

"I'm beginning to believe that myself — but the lady just might have other ideas." He studied his mother's countenance. "I'd hate to disappoint you."

They walked into the house together, and Brady dialed Charity's number.

"Charity, I'm glad you're there." Brady tried to keep his voice level. "Could I get a copy of the records you showed me? Good. I'll be there at seven-thirty p.m. and meet you at your office."

"I'm scared, Brady. I'm really scared."

"Hey, Doctor Fuller! Don't sound so deflated! I'm sure I want to go through with this. Cheer up. I'll see you at seven-thirty then, and we'll take a moonlight ride into the wide blue yonder." Brady chuckled and hung up.

Charity hesitated before she hung up the phone, Brady's voice lingering in her ears. "Oh, Brady Collins, you blind man. I love you. When will you wake up."

The rest of Charity's day soared away on wings of anticipation, and at closing time, she locked her office quickly. She had things to do to herself before Brady came.

Delicately perfumed, makeup glowing but natural, Charity looked at the clock eagerly. Six-thirty. An hour to wait. She locked her apartment and returned to the office. As she arrived, she stopped short as Sergeant Mayfield stepped out of nowhere and accosted her.

"Having trouble getting into your office? Here, let me help you." Mayfield grabbed her by the arm as he opened the door and pushed her inside. "See what the cat drug in." His gloating voice held a sneer.

Charity stumbled to the center of the room. As she gained her balance and saw the general sitting at her desk, she exploded.

"What is going on here?"

"Good evening, Dr. Fuller. Your unexpected arrival puts a different slant on the business at hand." General Freeman's voice was cool, but sweat was beading on his forehead.

"So this is a welcoming committee?" Fuller faced him, outraged.

"We like to be hospitable to our favorite employees, Fuller." His sourness contorted his face.

"Get to the point, general. I have work to do." Charity

stepped to her desk, and Freeman came to his feet menacingly.

"The point is this, Doctor Fuller. You and your boyfriend Collins have gone too far. When people start to believe the junk you two are pushing, things must change." The general stepped in front of Charity and grabbed her chin ferociously.

"Let go of me, you maniac!" She fought to get away.

"So, I'm a maniac now. You've called me a lot of things in the two years we've worked together but never this," he leered. "I never really thought it would come to this, but now that it has, I think I'm looking forward to it." Blood dripped from her mouth into his hand as he pushed her backward.

"You're a fool, Freeman. You can't get away with this, you know." Charity tried to bluff her way out.

"Well, we shall see." Calling to Mayfield, he commanded, "Get Curtis. When I'm through with her, take her to her apartment and see that this is the end."

Charity saw lust leap into the blue eyes of the general, and as he forced her against the storage shelves, she felt helpless.

"Don't be stupid, Freeman. Brady is telling the whole story to a reporter right now." Charity fought for time as her hand searched for a large glass she knew was there. "Collins and I will leave here, and there will be no trouble."

"No deal, sweet Charity. If those papers are burned and no Fuller to talk, I have no fears."

Charity's aim was true, and the force of her throw made the glass dig into the general's face as it shattered. His words turned into an oath, and a yell tore the air as both hands went to his bleeding face.

Almost instantly the door opened as Mayfield and Curtis rushed in just in time to block Charity's escape.

As Freeman recovered from the onslaught, his face still

bleeding, he barked, "Take her to her apartment, Mayfield. And do the job right."

"Your face, sir?" Mayfield looked with horror at Freeman.

"You do as I say and make it good. I'll attend to my face." His eyes glistened. "Collins could be showing before long, and this must be done before he comes."

"Yes, sir!" Mayfield and Curtis each took an arm. "One false move, Fuller, and bingo! Your arms are broken."

As Brady's car screeched to a halt at the check post, a flurried, ill-at-ease guard stepped in front of his car.

"Going to a fire, Collins?" The guard's shifty eyes made Brady uneasy.

"I am in a hurry, O'Toole — have a date with a blonde." Brady watched the guard, trying to sense any unusual interest but could not.

"Oh, Doctor Fuller. Well, well, this is interesting. She must have stood you up for a better guy. She passed through here about half an hour ago."

"Are you sure?"

"It's my job, Mr. Collins, to know who passes through here. Charity Fuller hasn't returned." The guard blustered.

"If you'll please step aside, I think I'll go to the office and wait. She knew I was coming." Brady lost his smile.

"If she comes, I'll tell her you're waiting." The guard moved grudgingly aside.

"You do that, O'Toole, and thanks." Brady shouted back at the guard as he roared away.

Brady stopped before the office building and dashed down the hall. Seeing Charity's door ajar and the light on, he halted, then tip-toed to the door. His intended greeting turned into shock.

"What is going on here!" Brady saw the broken beaker glass on the floor. "Charity!" Half-crazed he rushed to the sofa and as fresh blood marred the cloth, he touched it with his fingers, his mind in a whirl. Looking about, he noticed papers scattered about the floor and the desk in shambles. Sickening thoughts made cold sweat ooze profusely from his body, and his hands went wet and clammy. Trying to comprehend the situation, Brady hoped Charity would be in her apartment. He shook his head negatively and dared not to think what he might find.

Acting with caution, he slipped to the door and looked carefully about. Seeing his way clear, he hurried to the car and with as little noise as possible drove to Charity's apartment and circled around to her back door. Cutting the motor, Brady coasted in close. Slipping from the car, he tapped lightly on her door and tried to turn the knob.

"Charity," his whisper was anxious. "Charity! Charity!" His feeling for haste made him run around to the front entrance of the building, and in his hurry he wasn't alert enough to notice Mayfield and Curtis vanishing into the dark shadows of the hall. When he tried the door, it opened to his touch. He smelled gas fumes!

"Charity!" Brady's cry was a plea as his eyes took in the signs of struggle. Not finding her, he rushed to her bedroom and stiffened at the sight that met his eyes. A fire had been started in her bedroom. There, in a small pool of blood, her eyes glazed and half open, Charity's body lay beaten and bruised on the floor.

"Charity! What have they done to you?" Brady cradled her head against his chest. "Oh, my beautiful Charity, you can't be dead!" He smelled more gas. Knowing the place would explode any minute, Brady picked up Charity's limp body and rushed outside to the car. As he was speeding away, the whole building seemed to explode with fire. After a distance, he stopped the car. Taking Charity's limp arm, his fingers sought her pulse. Again and again his fingers probed for a sign of life. With a gasp he moaned, "She's alive! — just barely — but alive."

Putting a blanket over her in the back seat, Brady then roared the engine and sped toward Las Vegas. Brady stepped on the gas, hoping the law would come to his aid. His desires were quickly granted, and in a few moments a siren cleared the way into the emergency entrance of the hospital where a crew stood alerted and waiting.

It seemed hours as Brady tried to answer the questions of the police. And after giving his story, he said, "There will be some top officials at the test site investigated. I personally didn't see anything, but I know enough to pop the lid off this nuclear testing." He looked desperate. "Is there anything you can do?"

"No, this is government business. It's under military jurisdiction. I'm sorry," came the response from the detective.

Two hours passed before Brady was called into the intensive care unit. He could hardly believe what he saw as he looked at Charity; she was breathing. Enough color had returned to erase the look of death in her face, even though tubes and an oxygen tent made it still look serious. The bruises on her face had turned purple, one eye was black, and one arm was in a cast. What they had done to her insides he couldn't tell.

"What can you tell me about her condition?" Brady asked the nurse attendant hesitantly.

"Three broken ribs, a concussion, some internal bleeding." The nurse checked the tubes, felt the pulse, then listened to her heart. "She's steadily gaining, but her condition is still critical. By morning she should be all right."

"Not before then!" Brady exclaimed.

"It's a miracle she's alive. Just be thankful she's still here." The nurse looked at Brady and asked calmly, "Are you family?"

"No, not really."

"You may come back any time, Mr. —?" Her eyes were upon him.

"Collins. Brady Collins."

"Brady." The nurse smiled. "If she comes to, I'll tell her you brought her here."

"Thanks," Brady spoke quietly. He looked searchingly at the nurse. "You're sure she's going to make it?"

"She'll make it," the nurse assured him.

As Brady stood looking at Charity, a rush of love so penetrating and deep it made him weak swept over him. This feeling now far surpassed anything he had ever known. "My dear, sweet Charity. Just you get well, and somehow we'll even the score with whoever did this to you. I promise." Then he turned and walked out of the room.

CHAPTER 18

As Brady came out to the open night air of Las Vegas, he stood immobile and deep in thought. Suddenly, he whirled and made west on Charleston to Decatur then turned north to Smoke Ranch Road and west to a large estate almost standing alone. This was the home of Neal Crayton, a long-time friend of the family. As he drove in, one blast from the horn brought a big man out.

"Brady Collins, are you lost?" A strong hand went out in greeting.

"Not quite, Neal, but I've been busy. In fact, I'm in a sweat right now and came to ask a favor." Brady shook hands and then proceeded to tell his story.

"Whew! That bad?" Neal exclaimed after listening intently. "I hope you can do something. Is there anything I can do?"

"Well, I need to borrow a car and leave mine here," Brady asked.

"Sure you can take any one of my cars — just name it, and it's yours," Neal replied.

It wasn't long before Brady was on Tonopah Highway again, speeding to Mercury. As he approached the compound, the guard came out with a flourish.

"Well, well, Mr. Collins. Didn't recognize the car." The guard looked curious.

"You again, O'Toole?" Brady tried to be nonchalant. "Had trouble — had to park my car."

Brady moved inside the compound, each step calculated. He checked Charity's section of the compound to see the extent of activity her disappearance had caused. It being midnight and him in a strange car made his maneuvers less suspicious. Guards were thick about the building. Curtis and Mayfield were darting in and out excitedly, but there was no General Freeman.

Brady circled back and headed out as if to leave Mercury for Vegas. But instead, in an inconspicuous spot shaded by darkness and close to an alley, he parked and sat watching intently for all activity.

When the action outside had died down, he moved slowly and cautiously to the window of Charity's office. Testing it, it moved to his touch and slowly went up as he lifted. Looking about and seeing all was quiet, he jumped up on the sill and climbed through.

Not wanting to turn on the light, he pulled the drapes back just enough to let in the light from the moon. Going to where he knew Charity hid the key to her cabinet and with the aid of a little flashlight he carried on his key ring, he soon had the papers Charity had shown him before. Suddenly he froze. Lights came on in the adjoining office, and Freeman's voice was unmistakable. Closing and locking the cabinet, he glided softly to the connecting door and listened intently as he put the papers under his arm.

"Most unfortunate we had to lose Fuller. Are you sure you did a good job?" Freeman sounded skeptical. "Sorry in a way to

lose such a capable worker. She was the best I have ever worked
with." He paused, "One of the top people in her field."

"Yes, sir, I know — and a good-looking woman, if I may say
so. Boy was she a handful, strong as an ox. It took the two of us
to do the job," Mayfield boasted with a chuckle.

"If Collins hadn't rapped on the back, we could have had
time to get rid of the body," Curtis lamented.

"Are you sure he didn't see you?" Freeman's voice was
sharp.

"Not a chance. We were out the door and down the hall."

"Well, I hope you're right. This can't get out."

"What are you going to do about that Collins guy? He's the
stickler," Mayfield asked.

"Nothing," Freeman's voice was smooth. "That is, just yet.
Let things die down for a while; then we'll cancel him out just
like Dr. Phillips. He was finding out too much for his own good
and mine. I knew you were the men for the job."

"We understand," came Mayfield's voice. "Tonight has
been nasty, but now we hope to get the papers we need."

Brady felt the papers under his arm and grinned while
thinking how to get out of the office undetected. He was
unprepared for the front door of Charity's office to open.

"We'll break open Fuller's filing cabinet and. . . ,"
Freeman's voice froze as he flipped on the light to Charity's
office.

Shocked, Brady leaped to the window and nearly fell while
losing the papers in his haste.

"After him, Mayfield! Curtis! This time get him," Freeman
shouted.

Brady made for the parked car. But seeing Mayfield was too
close, bolted by it, not wanting him to know that was the one he

was driving. Head spinning, he ducked into the alley. Too late he saw it led nowhere, and being hemmed in, Brady spun round to fight his pursuers.

Brady realized it was his turn to feel the onslaught of the two sergeants he knew had mangled Charity. Watching them closely, he taunted, "Brave boys. Killing one little woman."

"Shut up!" roared Mayfield. "She asked for it!"

"Yah, big boys must take orders from a yellow-bellied general. He's too much of a skunk to do his own dirty work." Brady saw the rage twist his assailants' faces. "And you, Curtis. I hate a black-faced liar. You'd sell your soul for another stripe on your uniform."

"Shut him up, Mayfield," Curtis whined. "I don't like this kind of business. I told you a little brawl but no killing."

"Come on," Mayfield hissed. "Let's do it."

Mayfield advanced, hunched to attack. Brady side-stepped his charge and kicked over a garbage can that sent the first sergeant sprawling.

"Curtis, you lousy fool. Get him."

Brady stood solid, ready for Curtis. But before Curtis could lunge, Mayfield slid up behind Brady and cracked his skull with a leather-bound black-jack he carried on his belt.

"I've got him, Curtis!" Mayfield shrieked.

As Curtis looked at Brady's gapping head, he wrenched violently and slid to the ground.

"Why you fool. No guts, huh? Well, I've wanted to lay my hands on Collins for a long time." Mayfield, crazed with vengeance, began kicking Brady in the back and abdomen. Each blow registered a sickening dull thud. "Stop!" Curtis groaned. "Don't keep beating a dead man."

"Think he's done, Curtis?" Mayfield smirked.

"Yah, let's get him behind these boxes."

As they finished, just then a guard car went by, and a light started to flash up the alley. The two spirited for cover.

"Close call!" Mayfield laughed at his victory. "Let's get out of here. We'll move Collins later tonight when the coast's clear."

Brady groaned and stirred. He tried to move but blanked out again. Again he came to, and this time flashes of remembrance came lucid to his mind. He knew he'd lost the valued papers, and he moaned again.

Slowly he tried to get up but fell back, panting for breath. Gaining his wind, he slowly hitched himself down the alley. Waves of nauseating pain tore through him from every direction. After an hour of torture, he somehow found himself at the back door of his apartment. Dragging himself along, he made it to the door and let himself in.

Brady pulled the phone down and managed to dial "0."

"Operator," Mildred's voice was reassuring. "Operator!" came the voice more pronounced.

"Mildred," Brady's voice was agonized.

"Brady?"

"I — I need help," Brady gasped.

"Brady, listen. I'm off in ten minutes. Hang on, please. Should I call a guard?" Mildred sounded hysterical.

"No. Th—e-y'-d kill. . . ." The phone went dead in her ear.

Mildred let herself into Brady's room, and as she saw him, a cry of horror leaped from her lips. "Brady, what happened!"

"Get me — into — the back — of — that. . .that blue car. Cover me. Get me — to this address in Vegas." Brady pushed some scribbled words and numbers at her.

"But why? Let me call the general."

119

"No! Just do as I say. Trust me."

Brady passed out momentarily but woke to find himself between the seats of his car. Mildred soon had pillows and quilts over him and made for the highway.

As she came to the check guard, he grinned at her. "Not driving the Volkswagon today?"

"Emergency. Had to borrow this one."

The guard waved her through.

Mildred drove into the yard at the address Brady gave her, and a man came forward, a grimace on his face.

"How did you get my car?" The man looked menacingly at her.

"Brought a friend here — help us." Mildred sprang out, shaking, and nervously opened the back door to expose Brady's split head.

"What happened?" The man looked like an angry bull ready to charge.

Mildred sobbed out all she knew complete with the instructions of no guards.

Two days later Brady came to in a cool, pleasant hospital room. He tried to get up, but a strong hand pinned him fast.

"Not yet, Brady boy. You've had a very narrow escape," Neal Crayton's voice came assuringly. "You're safe here."

"Charity? I've got to go to Charity!" Brady struggled.

"Now hold it, Brady. She's coming along fine." Neal grinned. "Your ramblings gave us enough clues — we found her."

"Is she. . . ?"

"Sure, she's okay. Out of intensive care and getting about." Neal tossed a quizzical glance, "She's mighty interested in you."

Brady grinned sheepishly as he fell back against the pillows. "How did you manage all this?"

"Your friend Mildred brought you," Neal's voice came with assurance. "And you know Walter Cox. He's a few years older than you but a home-towner. He's one of the top doctors here — the rest was easy."

"Thanks, Neal." Brady puckered his brow. "I remember calling Mildred, and that's it."

"That gal has guts; she's crazy about you, too." Neal laughed. "Do they all come running at the snap of your fingers, Brady?"

"Naw — but this time I'm glad one did." Brady grinned, then turned serious. "How long am I here for?"

"Well, doc says it will take time, but there's nothing that won't mend. I have instructions to keep you quiet. Doc will be here tonight, and it's up to him. Just take it easy today."

"Anyone else know I'm here?" Brady looked anxiously at Neal.

"No. I quizzed two of my buddies that work out at Mercury. All seems quiet out there."

"They won't like it, Charity and me both surviving." A worried frown creased his brow.

"That's not important yet, Brady, but this is. Doctor Fuller's father and mother flew in from D.C. It seems they are in with the top brass back there." Neal grinned. "It's all undercover their being here. Seems this Charity gal has been opening up to them for some time, and they're anxious to meet you."

"And General Freeman?" Brady paused. "Has he tried to contact Charity?"

"I don't think so. Now get some rest."

"I'll be fine. Neal, I really owe you one."

"No, Brady. It's we who live here who owe you. Keep fighting."

CHAPTER 19

Sarah Collins peeked anxiously into Brady's room and jerked as usual at the sight of her son's smooth, half-shaved head and the bandages that covered it. After the initial shock of seeing her battered son, gratitude filled her heart that he was still alive.

But before she could say anything, the telephone shrilled through the house, and Sarah hurriedly picked it up.

"Hello! — Oh, he's doing a lot better. — Yes, he was brought home Saturday, but he's slept for nearly two days. Listen, Francis, I'll call you back, okay?"

Sarah looked again into the room and found Brady awake and getting up from the bed.

"Mom?"

"Yes, Brady dear."

"Mom, your fears about the nuclear bombs — they *are* killing innocent people. They *know* it, and I *know* it, just as surely as they tried to kill me." Brady brushed his hand across his eyes. "That is, General Freeman does. Now whether Washington knows, I'm not sure, but I'm going to find out."

"Listen, dear, you've been through a lot; can't we talk later? You shouldn't get too excited."

"Mom, I just can't sit still and let that two-faced culprit go on with his murdering," Brady lashed out. "Mom, that man is a lunatic — I can't let him make lab rats out of people any longer."

"Brady, you're so much like your father. Will you never give up?" Tears were close to the surface.

"How's Dad doing, anyway?" Brady wasn't sure if his mother would tell the truth. But she did.

"Not too good. It's so cruel seeing him waste away by inches. He's nothing but skin and bones." Sarah patted his hand. "Oh, Brady, I forgot to ask you about Charity. Shouldn't we call her?" Sarah asked eagerly.

"She's in the hospital, Mom."

"What? Did she get hurt with you?" Anxiety touched her voice.

"No — but the same people tried to kill her who tried to put an end to me." Brady grew pensive. "Mom, I want to ask a favor."

"It's about Charity. When she's released — could she come here?" Brady watched his mother's face.

"But, of course. I'd really like to know her better. She's a lovely young woman." Eagerness made her eyes sparkle.

"Yes, she is beautiful. And, Mom, I've already asked her to come here. I knew what you'd say." Brady let out his breath in relief. "You're an angel."

"When will you bring her?" Sarah's face showed anticipation.

"Perhaps next week. Her parents came out for a few days but couldn't stay. They are doctors, too. Mrs. Fuller is one of the leading pathologists at the Walter Reed Hospital, and Mr. Fuller is one of the head surgeons there. I wonder if they would ever accept me? They are pretty hot stuff."

"Now, dear, your lady isn't like that at all. No need to think her parents are." She tried to console him. "You bring her here, and we'll love her back to health."

"I'm going back to Vegas tomorrow — I must see her again."

"No, you can't do that. You're still a bit shaky and not that well yet for driving long distances. Call her now and talk to her; let her decide. I'm sure she wouldn't want you to endanger yourself." Sarah arose. "Go to my bedroom and call. You'll find some privacy there." Turning back to her son, her face showed signs of concern. "Dear, did you meet Charity's parents?"

"Yes, they came to the hospital while I was there and got my story. They also thanked me for saving their daughter's life."

The next day Brady was half awake, and the first fingered rays of a new dawn were barely breaking through the window when the entire house was suddenly illuminated. Throwing the covers off quickly, Brady half staggered to the kitchen window and looked south and a little west. Out of the corner of his eye he noticed a figure hunched in a chair.

"Mom?"

"Yes, dear."

"You're crying?"

"These terrible explosions just aren't any good. In a few minutes you'll hear the swish like the wind coming, then the house will tremble. Oh, Brady, if that were all, I wouldn't care. But in a few hours that horrible cloud will come." She wiped her eyes.

The two stood motionless for a few moments, each deep in thought.

"Listen! Here it comes!" Sarah's eyes were large.

Brady shivered. "It's like an earthquake!"

Sarah finally spoke. "Well, it's over, at least for now."

"Brady, dear, a neighbor comes early to do the chores, and I'm always up. You go back to bed. You need the rest. We want you on your feet when Charity comes."

Brady slept soundly until his mother's voice, full of anxiety and fear, brought him fully awake.

"Jeremy, Jenny, it's here again! Don't just stand there! Come inside, quickly."

"Mama, it's low, isn't it?" Young Jenny squinted as she looked at the very low grey cloud.

"Yes, it's *too* low." Hysteria filled her mind. "Oh, someone, please release us from all this agony!"

"Mom, how many clouds this low have you had here?" Brady stood pale and shaking.

"Several, but this may be the lowest." Sarah sounded stoic and listened to the radio blaring its usual warning.

"Attention to all St. George residents and those in the vicinity. Go indoors and shut off all ventilation from outside. Every precaution is being used to safeguard you and your families. There is no danger."

Why that dirty, low-down. . . . Even a snakepit is too good for you, Freeman, Brady thought to himself white hot with anger.

"Oh, Brady, I do a lot of talking to my maker at night. Often I stand by my window or go out into the night and look into heaven. My heart runs over, and I cry for help. The Lord will help us, I know."

"But, Mom, the Lord commands us to help ourselves, too."

"I know. You're right." Her smile was gentle. "There will

come a reckoning. It may take time, but it will come."

That afternoon Brady was resting in the hammock on the front lawn when a jeep drove into the yard. Two men got out, and going to the back, took out Geiger counters and other paraphernalia. Their talk was loud, and the word radiation brought Brady swinging to his feet.

"Hey, you two! You're on private ground!" Brady drew their attention to him. "What are you doing here?"

"Brady Collins! What in the world are you doing in St. George?" A stout, sandy-haired man extended his hand.

"Gus Thompson!" Brady shook hands with gusto. "The last I saw you, you were at Alamogordo base."

"Yah, you went to Denver, and I've been going wherever the government has a sticky job." He grinned. Turning to his companion, he said, "Brady, this is Wesley Long. We've been sent to run some tests. The mayor from here called the test site this morning and did some threatening. Said they had tough information they were going to print if something wasn't done about the fallout. He said the cloud was low enough to touch."

"You've been at the site?" Brady looked stunned.

"For two weeks. I came in with a Doctor — what's his name — McFee, I think. I don't know what his job is." Gus frowned. "What happened to you? Someone want you dead?"

Brady bit his tongue. He wasn't too sure this was the time to explode his own bomb. "I had a run-in with some people. I'll tell you about it some other time. You said you're here to run tests? How long you going to stay?"

"A few days. We have designated areas, Southern Utah, Nevada, and a little in Arizona," Gus grinned.

"What do you expect to find?" Brady forced a smile.

"Brady, you know what without asking. And I know, too. But we can't open our mouths." Gus seemed uneasy. "You didn't answer my question, Brady. How'd you get messed up?"

"Come around some other day, Gus. It's a long story."

"Okay. Well, have to report back to General Freeman."

"Yah, he's quite a general," Brady quipped. "Gets what he wants, too, one way or another."

"Sounds like you know him pretty good. Can't say as I like this new doctor too much either. He's hard to figure. Anything for a fast buck, I'd say." Putting out his hand, Brady shook it. "Get well, pal. We'll see each other again."

"Yah, I'll be seeing you. And, Gus, make those reports good. I'd say better duplicate them. Sometimes valuable reports get lost."

"No chance, Brady. They go directly to Freeman and from him, who knows." Gus looked sharply at Brady, then continued. "You know — it used to be there had to be two reports, one for the man in charge and one for the scientist, but not now."

"I still say a copy in your own files would be smart," Brady shot his friend a hard look.

"Thanks for your suggestion, Brady. See ya around."

Brady stared after them until they were out of sight and then walked back into the house, wondering what his next move should be.

CHAPTER 20

Charity Fuller had been at the farm with the Collins' for two weeks now, and the ease with which she fit into their way of life amazed her. Their real sincerity came easy from them — nothing was forced or stilted. Their way of life was simple and refreshing.

Jeremy and young Jenny were a marvel to her, too. Never having had a real home filled with love but rather being tutored from infancy in the higher academics, Charity had always put precision and achievement above all else. As she watched the love ricochet from one member of the family to the other, it was young Jenny who captivated her heart most. Hardly six, her little fingers flew over the piano keys almost as fast as a smile could light up her face and the faces of anyone around her.

Each day brought new awakenings in Charity's soul to what family togetherness meant. Even Brady basked in the glow of his mother's love and devotion. His awareness of things to be done, even menial tasks about the house, impressed her greatly. Charity found his presence soothing. He seemed to sense her every need even before she did herself. Many times she had started a sentence only to have it finished by him. And, at first to her chagrin, she caught herself doing the same with him.

Brady had laughed at her. "It's a benediction, Charity; just don't thwart it."

At first, she didn't understand. But little by little comprehension dawned, and a radiance new to her opened horizons that almost made her gasp.

"Don't fight it; let it blossom and grow," she reminded herself. Brady's actions were natural and easy.

"Brady, I do love your family, even more than my own. Until now, love had held a different meaning. Success, fame, education were synonymous with love." Charity relaxed in his arms.

"We are just an ordinary family, and you at first seemed so unattainable." Brady kissed her gently. "Charity, I'm still a bit afraid of your parent's disapproval. They are so — so. . . ."

"So formidable," she laughed. "Very efficient, too; yes, it's the years of being in command. But, Brady, they make a great team and get along famously." With a twinkle in her eyes she spoke low. "They've already discerned my feelings toward you, and from what they could see of you they like you, too. Remember, Brady, you saved my life."

"Whew!" Brady pretended to stagger. "That takes a load off my mind."

"And by the way, Mr. Collins, Dad and Mother have rounded up Dr. Wilcox and Dr. Mathews and have put our stories with theirs. It seems they even put some of the top generals in Washington on the spot. They are a little jittery right now." Charity let out a sigh. "When they start the ball rolling, it's hard to say where it will stop." She paused, brows creased. "Mother and Dad believe these tests should go on but in a different way."

"I do, too!" Brady spoke up quickly, "but not Freeman's way."

"Come on, Brady. Let's get dinner for your Mom. She'll be home from the hospital soon." Together they enjoyed the cooking, and Charity smiled contentedly. "A year ago if someone had told me I'd be bending over a stove, I'd have laughed outright and called him stupid; but now look at me!"

Meanwhile, outside the Collins' farm, a government car with its lights off slowly drove up the long dirt road to the house. Two figures got out and crept stealthfully to the back door. They peered in the window and saw Brady and Charity in the kitchen.

"That Fuller lady *is* alive, Mayfield," Curtis whispered. "I thought we had finished her off."

"Well, we'll finish them *both* off now and forever," Mayfield smirked as he pulled out a revolver and grasped the latch to the door.

The two men bolted through the door and surprised Brady and Charity. Charity let out a scream and clutched Brady's arm.

"Just hold it right there. Thought you could get away from us, huh?" Mayfield leered. "We've been lookin' for you, Collins, for two weeks, but after overhearing a private conversation from a new guy out at the test site about you being here, we decided to check it out, and we hit the jackpot. You won't be able to blab to any reporters now."

"You won't get away with this. . . ." Brady gritted his teeth.

"Shut up! You've made enough trouble for us already. General Freeman thinks you're both dead and that we cleaned up all the evidence. He'll never know the difference," Curtis interjected nervously.

"Check the place out, sergeant. Make sure nobody is

around. Then we'll take these two out in the desert and get the job finished," Mayfield ordered.

Curtis went from room to room and found the place empty.

"No one's here, Sarg. Let's go."

The two started to back up to the kitchen door just as it slowly opened behind them.

"Freeze, busters, right in your tracks and drop those guns," commanded Sarah Collins gruffly, holding a shotgun.

"Mother!" exclaimed Brady.

"I thought there was something fishy when I saw a car turn off its lights coming up to the house. I was just coming home from the hospital and guess I hit my timing right," Sarah added.

"Where did you get that shotgun?" Brady asked as he picked up the guns that were dropped.

"Your father keeps this out in the back shed." Sarah pointed to the two sergeants to raise their hands. "Don't try anything, you two; this thing is loaded to the hilt."

"Charity, call Sheriff Donner and tell him to get over here quick!" Brady said, "I'll hold these two till he comes. They're going to have a lot of explaining to do."

"Freeman ordered us to take care of things — it wasn't our idea," exclaimed Mayfield. "We just. . . ."

Brady cut him off. "We know who is behind all this. You're all going to be locked up for a long time."

Sheriff Donner quickly arrived and heard the entire story from Brady. The sheriff handcuffed the two men and drove them into town.

Charity hugged Brady after the frightening ordeal was over, and then they both hugged Sarah for saving them.

"I didn't believe what I saw, Mother!" Brady exclaimed.

Sarah Collins was still shaking. "I didn't believe it either, but I had to do what had to be done," she replied with a nervous smile.

They all hugged each other again, knowing their lives had been spared.

CHAPTER 21

T he night was warm, and a full moon played hide-and-seek poking through and then disappearing. Charity Fuller wasn't used to romantic evenings on a farm. She could hear the gurgling of the water in the small stream near the farm house as she and Brady rocked in the swinging chair on the front porch.

Everything about the night seemed perfect. Brady had thought a lot about *the question* he was going to ask, yet doing it wasn't as easy as he'd anticipated. He figured by talking more would ease his nervousness. Brady formulated his plan.

"Charity — I like the proposal your folks talked about from Senator Lowell about us working for him in his investigation of the tests and all. He wants people with technical background. We could blow the whole lid off this thing and stay right here." Brady fumbled for words.

Charity just sat there, not saying a word.

"You weren't thinking of going back East were you? You like it here, don't you?" he asked inquisitively.

"Brady, what are you trying to say?"

He looked into Charity's eyes and thought he'd better say it now. "Charity, would you consider marrying me and staying here on the farm for awhile? We can recuperate here — we can work here for the Senator — and we could. . . ."

Charity laughed, cutting Brady's words short. "You aren't giving me a chance to say, YES!"

Brady nearly fell off the chair. He stood up and pulled Charity up to him. She hugged him tight.

"Oh, Brady. I do love you," she said emotionally. "After the experiences we've been through, I don't want to ever leave you."

Brady lovingly kissed her.

The romantic evening calm was shattered by Sarah Collins' frantic voice.

"Brady! Oh, Brady!" his mother's wail took him to her side almost instantly.

"What is it, Mother?"

"Brady, it's the hospital. When I left your father at six o'clock, he looked good. Now he's turned to the worst." Sarah wept openly.

"Mother, we'll take you to the hospital," Brady said softly as he gently took his mother in his arms. "I'll get Mrs. Taylor to come stay with the twins."

Within a few moments they were on their way with Charity tucked in between them. Brady knew this wasn't the best conclusion for a romantic evening as it started out to be or to even tell his mother of their decision. There would be time later for that.

As the three entered Jed's room, his breathing was erratic and laborious. Looking at him, they sensed he was beyond the point of return.

"Mrs. Collins, your husband went into a coma just minutes before I called." The nurse was grave and spoke in short bursts.

"I'll bring another chair. I'm sure you'll wish to remain."

Brady left with the nurse and returned with an easy chair. The nurse came back with an arm full of newspapers.

"Here, you can scan the papers. It will help pass the time. There's really nothing anybody can do."

The night passed, and Jedediah Collins still struggled for life. Charity browsed through the newspapers until her eyes lit on an article of interest.

"Brady!" Excitement broke softly from Charity's lips as she read. "Listen to this: *'While there was no official rebuttals from the Atomic Energy Commission, it was learned from Washington today that the A.E.C. is taking a longer look at some of the alleged cover-ups by some heads of Army installations. A Congressional investigation initiated by Senators from Utah, Nevada, and Arizona has begun.'* Dad and Mother have pulled some strings! Brady, there's more: *'It has been brought to the attention of the Defense Command in Washington that physical beatings at the Nuclear Test Site had been ordered to suppress damaging evidence from leaking out. It is reported that two army sergeants from the test site were arrested in St. George, Utah, in connection with the alleged beatings and have confessed to a wide scale cover-up and conspiracy.'*" Charity excitedly held out the paper to Brady.

"Charity, look!" Brady pointed a finger to an article tucked away in the corner of the newspaper. They read together: *'Acting with celerity, Army Headquarters has issued orders for the removal of its leading officer at the test site and a possible court-martial is pending, according to a reliable source in Nevada.'*

"Well, well, your parents *do* have power back in Washington," Brady smiled.

"Yes, to a certain extent. They could get quick action towards Freeman's hatchet men, but it'll be slower for the general. A court-martial and a prison sentence are too good for Freeman. They ought to make him drink all the milk from the dairies in St. George as punishment!" Charity laughed.

Charity stopped laughing as the hospital was illuminated by a brilliant light.

Brady quickly looked at Charity, and their eyes flashed with anger. Another detonation!

"That test wasn't supposed to go off until next week!" exclaimed Brady. "I'll bet Freeman ordered it for sheer spite and his ego!"

Charity rose slowly to her feet and walked over to Jedediah's bedside. Brady came up behind her and took her hand in his. A swishing sound came, and almost instantly the wind followed, and the building trembled just as Jed's last breath of life escaped his body.

"Brady, he's gone!" Sarah wept as she held onto Jed's limp hand, trying to will it back to life.

Brady took his mother into his arms and cradled her close. "It's all right, Mom. It's better this way." He tried to make her smile as tears welled up in his eyes.

"I know. Yes. I know, but — it's so. . . ," Sarah nearly crumpled, then straightened. "It will be so very hard without him."

Brady held his mother up and tried to comfort her.

"I want you to know your father loved you dearly, Brady." Sarah looked into her son's moist eyes.

Charity turned and awkwardly walked from the room, a stifled sob echoing behind her. Brady quickly followed her out and slipped his arm around her.

"Charity. Everything will be okay. Dad wanted us to be happy."

"Oh, Brady. It's true. This whole awful — destructive — mess. It's killed your father, and I don't know how many others." Charity sobbed in his arms.

"What will come tomorrow we may be able to change. We'll do it for Dad. Let's go get Mom and leave here."

They slowly left the room with Sarah and walked down the long hallway. They passed the nurse's station and overheard the radio announcement on the way out: '*We interrupt this program for a special announcement. Another atomic test has been successfully conducted at the United States Nuclear Test Site, and the residue-carrying cloud is expected to pass over St. George in approximately two hours. There is no need to fear if the residents take the following, simple precautions. . . .*'

The wheels to expose the truth were beginning to slowly grind forward. Brady and Charity knew now their fight had just begun.